eXistenZ

Christopher Priest

↔

based on the screenplay by
David Cronenberg

↔

HarperEntertainment
A Divison of HarperCollinsPublishers

HarperEntertainment
A Division of HarperCollins*Publishers*
10 East 53rd Street, New York, NY 10022-5299

This is a work of fiction. The characters, incidents, and
dialogues are products of the author's imagination and are not to
be construed as real. Any resemblance to actual events or
persons, living or dead, is entirely coincidental.

ISBN 0-06-102027-3

A massmarket edition of this book was published in
Great Britain in 1999 by Simon & Schuster U.K.

First HarperEntertainment printing: May 1999
Printed in the United States of America

Visit HarperEntertainment on the World Wide Web at
http://www.harpercollins.com

❖ 10 9 8 7 6 5 4 3 2 1

[1]

Something buzzed and fluttered against Ted Pikul's chest, feeling like a large winged insect. With his mind on other things, he swiped at it absently, flapping his fingers with an irritated motion across the crisply starched fabric of his shirt. In the dark it was impossible to see if anything flew or dropped away from him, but the insistent drumming of the wings ceased.

Pikul took a deep breath in the warm night air and for the tenth time in as many minutes stared apprehensively around at the vehicles crammed into the weed-overgrown parking lot.

Only a dim overhead lamp illuminated the vehicles, creating a large but pallid pool of light around the ones closest to the entrance to the old church hall. The vehicles were almost all of the sort you'd see in any small country town: most were pickups and trucks streaked with mud or rust, or both, and many had doors or fenders held on with wire. Great rolls of chicken wire, anonymous-looking plastic sacks, or battered agricultural implements were heaped on the flatbeds behind the drivers' cabs.

One vehicle stood out prominently in this undistinguished company: a gleaming late-model Land Rover Defender 110, which had seven seats, a roof cage, and a winch hanging off the front.

Sitting behind the wheel of this car was another Antenna Research employee, Frances McCarrigan, to whom Ted Pikul had been told to make himself known as soon as he arrived. He had done so. Frances, a retired lady farmer who sometimes picked up a few extra bucks moonlighting as a chauffeur, had acknowledged his arrival with an absent glare.

The thing buzzed once more, in the same place on his shirtfront. Pikul flapped anxiously at it, but this time remembered what he'd put in his pocket.

He reached in and pulled out the pink-fone. It vibrated a third time while he held it. He fumbled it around in his fingers and turned toward the dim light spilling through the doorway that led to the interior of the hall. The design of the pink-fone was so subtle and understated that it was difficult to work out which way it should be held. It was state-of-the-art palm-sized bioware, fashioned from the latest in modular thermoplastics and programmed with genetically enhanced enzyme circuitry. The plastic was soft, and felt warm to the touch.

He squeezed the sides, as he'd been shown by his boss, Alex Kindred, head of PR at Antenna Research. They squelched silently in his grip and a diffuse pink light swelled up from deep within it.

"Er—hello?" he said, into what he believed was the receiver.

"Pickle?" said a sharp voice against his ear. "Is that Theodore Pickle?"

"Er, no . . . I mean, yes it's me, I'm—"

"Put Pickle on. The security guard. Why the hell isn't he there?"

"Sir, it's me. Ted Pikul. The name rhymes with 'Michael.'"

"It's the Antenna security office here. You were supposed to call in at ten minute intervals. What the devil's going on out there?"

"Everything's under control, sir."

"Has Allegra Geller shown up?"

"Yes, sir," Pikul said, with a glance at the Land Rover. "She's taking part in the software presentation right now. With . . . with all the other representatives from Antenna. Sir."

"Don't call it software, Mr. Pikul. How long have you been with us?"

"Long enough to know the song," Pikul recited from the company manual. "I'm sorry, sir. I meant that she's presenting the game system."

"Okay, we always pay attention to detail at

Antenna. Now, why aren't you with her, Pikul? She's the one you're supposed to be protecting. You want me to send replacement security staff down there if you can't handle it?"

"No, sir. I can handle it okay. I've been following instructions, but I thought I should run one of my periodic checks on the outside of the location. I've surveyed the area, and confirmed that all our security expectations are in place. I was about to rejoin Ms. Geller when you called."

"Right. Check back in here in ten minutes. You got that, Pikul?"

"I got it. Sir."

The pink light faded from within the fone and Pikul carefully slipped the plastic instrument into his shirt pocket, trying to remember which way was up. The next time it buzzed he didn't want to have to fumble with it.

He pulled the electronic security wand from his belt, then stepped quickly across to the highway beyond the parking lot. He looked in both directions. To the right, leading south, the road ran off into indeterminate landscape; you couldn't see much in the light from the half-moon. To the north, a line of mountains ran jaggedly against the star-filled night sky.

It was a hot night, the warm winds blowing in from the hundreds of square miles of farmland that lay all around. Pikul looked wistfully at the shape of the distant mountains, thinking of cool air and crystal-clear mountain streams.

No cars were approaching from either direction, which was what he'd wanted to establish. Or at least, this was what he wanted to establish while he calmed down after the call from the head office.

With one more inhalation of the fragrant country air, and another pensive glance in the direction of the mountains, Pikul walked swiftly back to the building and made his way inside.

It had once been a simple country church, but was deconsecrated years ago. In recent times it had been used for dances, community meetings, elections, and the occasional political rally.

Pikul had been told the hall was typical of those where Antenna tested their product for market evaluation: it was in a remote country area with a high percentile of known Antenna users, the hall was familiar with everyone in the locality and was cheap to rent, and in addition it was an unobtrusive place for Antenna's top VR people to gather. You couldn't be too careful these days.

The whole interior was well-lit, but large mobile lights had been wheeled to the front to illuminate the platform at the far end.

Pikul spotted Allegra Geller standing at the back of

the crowd. She was dressed to blend. Her clothes were modest and conservative—a dark blue jacket over an Antenna Research T-shirt; slim jeans on her shapely legs; her hair was long and fair—but there was no disguising the sheer intelligence and beauty that radiated from her no matter how she stood, or spoke, or looked.

When he'd been briefly introduced to her, half an hour earlier as the Antenna people began arriving, Pikul could hardly believe his luck at being assigned to her on his first security commission. This was a first not only for him, but also something of a first for her too. Although Allegra Geller was famous, it was mostly through rumor and hearsay. She had rarely been allowed into public by Antenna, and apart from a few small photographs accompanying magazine articles carefully leaked over the last two years, her face was all but unknown. For both these reasons Pikul was in awe of her, even though the few words she'd uttered to him when they met had been friendly enough. So far. Pikul never doubted his unfortunate ability to say exactly the wrong thing at the wrong time.

He went and sat down in the chair that had been placed next to the main entrance. He laid his security wand across his lap.

The temperature had risen in the hall while he'd been outside: it was not only several degrees warmer, but the emotional atmosphere being pumped out by the crowd was noticeably more frenetic. Their responses had been deliberately whipped up from the platform by some rousing speeches and corporate displays; now they were ready for the product pitch.

One of the Antenna operatives, Wittold Levi, a man in his early forties, was standing to one side of the platform, facing the crowd. He held a short piece of white chalk. Next to him, a large chalkboard rested on a tripod.

Levi was playing on the expectations of the crowd, feeding on their waves of concentration. He rocked slightly on his heels.

"*eXistenZ*!" he said suddenly. "The word is *eXistenZ*!"

He turned to the chalkboard and with a swift rapping sound wrote the word in large letters. He spelled it out deliberately, tapping the end of the chalk against each letter.

"Always spell it this way," Levi said. "Small e, capital X, capital Z on the end." He turned back to the audience. "*eXistenZ* . . . it's new, it's hot, it's from Antenna Research, and it's here right now."

Everyone cheered and applauded enthusiastically, and Levi raised his face to catch the full beam of the twin spotlights, illuminating his face as if with inner radiance. He glanced enticingly across at the crowd: some people were still sitting in the rows of old wooden pews, or the uncomfortable plastic chairs brought in for the evening, but by now many were standing.

As the applause continued, Levi paced away from the chalkboard and with a measured tread stepped precisely toward the other side of the platform. He paused, turned, looked appreciatively out at the eager audience, then went back to the chalkboard. He timed it so the cheering and clapping faded as once again he stood at the center of the stage.

Behind him, on the other side of the platform, two young women assistants, obviously selected for their lovely faces and the way their figures filled out the trim outlines of the corporate designer relaxware, were carefully laying out some twenty or more plastic modules. From Pikul's view at the back of the room, the modules looked a little like high-tech ski boots.

Levi raised his hand, ensuring that complete silence fell.

"My name is Wittold Levi," he said, enunciating carefully. "My friends call me Witt . . . so I guess you can call me Witt too. I'm the project manager for *eXistenZ*, responsible for all development and customer input." He raised his hand to shield his eyes from the spotlights, and peered at some of the audience. "I see a whole lot of familiar faces out there . . . but that's okay. You can all hang around for the rest of the show."

The laughter was warm; many of them had seen Witt's work before.

"Antenna's entire corporate rationale is to encourage consumer loyalty, and that's why we're here

8

with you tonight. We need you, all of you, to help us with our product testing. We're a team, Antenna and you. Those of you who have been invited to one of our seminars before will know that I normally lead you through our new games myself. Tonight, though, Antenna is launching *eXistenZ*, and that makes it a special occasion. To show you how special, we have brought you a seminar leader who can only be described as . . . unique."

A ripple of anticipation moved through the crowd: people were swaying with excitement.

A young man standing close to Pikul said to a friend in an urgent whisper, "I don't believe it! They wouldn't bring her here! Not here!"

His companion's face was sheened with perspiration, and the muscles of his jaw visibly tightened.

"I don't know," he said. "I've been hearing rumors for weeks. Gee, I hope that's who he's talking about! But Allegra Geller in this no-horse town?"

Pikul glanced across at Allegra Geller, who had moved to where the refreshments had been laid out on a long table. She was helping herself to a cookie, but otherwise showed no reaction at all.

Witt grinned boyishly as he picked up on the whispered anticipation from the audience.

"Yes it is!" he said, and raised his hands as if to open the clouds. "The world's greatest game designer is here with you in person, tonight. It is your privilege that she will lead you, lead you herself, through her latest creation: *eXistenZ* from Antenna Research is here . . . "

Two people in the front row of the crowd fell to their knees, their faces burnished with excitement.

"Ladies and gentlemen, tonight I give you . . . the Game-Pod Goddess herself—Allegra Geller!"

Witt leaped from the platform, brushing between the two people on their knees. He pushed his way firmly but politely through the press of the crowd. People moved to make way for him, recognizing that something sensational was about to happen in their lives. Every face in the room turned to follow his progress across the room.

He strode directly toward Allegra Geller. She brushed a finger across her lips to wipe away any crumbs that might have adhered.

Witt paused before her, a knowing half smile on his face. He raised his hand to take hers, then turned to lead her back through the crowd toward the platform. People stepped aside in awe, almost like water parted by a miracle as she passed between them. She kept her gaze averted.

As she moved away from him, Pikul saw that what he'd assumed was a shoulder bag was in fact a game-pod case, supported on a long strap. The pod hung at her waist. She rested her hand on it in an apparently relaxed way, but Pikul noticed that no matter how much she twisted or leaned as she walked through the audience, her hand never once strayed from the pod.

He realized that the awestruck mood of the crowd was getting to him, distracting him. He had a job to do, and that was to protect the young woman. He left his chair and moved swiftly toward one side of the raised platform.

Allegra Geller followed Wittold Levi, her free hand still held lightly in his. Standing in the center of the platform, she seemed dazed by the lights and the reaction of her followers. Clearly, she was nervous, but her modest smiles made her seem, to Pikul at least, a vision of all that was good, wise, intelligent, and beautiful in the world.

He stared at her in rapt attention.

"Hi, everyone!" Allegra said with the flash of a natural smile, narrowing her eyes in the glare of lights. "I'm Allegra Geller."

The wave of warmth and the sheer enthusiasm of the applause that came back at her seemed to have a tangible pressure, because she rocked momentarily.

"Well, I'm glad to see so many of you were able to come here tonight."

They laughed appreciatively. It was a knowing joke, one she knew they were all in on. And it was one they knew she knew . . . When Antenna Research announced a new Geller product presentation, you called off lunch with the President to be there. Even if you didn't know Allegra Geller herself was going to be present.

"Let me give it to you straight," she continued, after a thoughtful pause. "The world of games is in a kind of trance. Most people are programmed to accept so little, but the possibilities are great. Infinite, in fact."

She paused to glance expressively around at the crowd, feeding on their response. They were so hyped up, they were practically humming with anticipation.

"Okay," Allegra said. "I see you've been thinking the same way I have. That's why you're here. You probably thought that tonight we were going to test a new game. One I designed. Is that right?"

There was a roar of assent.

"I'm sorry . . . there is no new game for you to test. At least, not in the usual sense."

She was starting to enjoy herself. While many people groaned with disappointment, Allegra looked winsomely at the bare boards of the platform floor, her eyes twinkling.

"No, I guess I can say that it's going to be much better than that! More than you expected. *eXistenZ* is not just a game." She had their attention again. She began pacing, to give emphasis to her words. "It's more than a game, it's a whole new game system. Antenna Research and I have developed it together—the *eXistenZ* System by Antenna—and it involves a whole lot of new toys. New experiences. New challenges. New insights into not only the world of reality, but into your own inner consciousness. Tonight you are going to be among the very first people in the world to try out these new systems."

Witt now stepped forward, chalk in hand.

"Yeah," he said over the excited noise. "I can second what Ms. Geller has said. The new Antenna Research game system is something you're going to hear a lot more about. It's called MetaFlesh."

He turned to the board and rapped out the letters of the word with the same flourish as before.

"It's written like this," he said, tapping at the letters. "Get it right, from the start. One word. Capital M, capital F. MetaFlesh is what our new games are made from . . . the MetaFlesh Game-Pod, only from Antenna Research. It connects with any industry standard bioport." He made a suggestive swerve of his hips and gave a knowing, sensual look at the crowd. "I realize you all have those bioports, or you wouldn't be here at all . . . "

They loved that. Possession of a bioport was clearly the entrance ticket to a whole range of sensual experiences, whose thrills could only be guessed at by those who had so far failed to get a bioport fitted.

People like Ted Pikul, who had so far failed to get a bioport fitted.

He glared at the crowd and tightened his grip on the electronic wand.

Witt was continuing. ". . . MetaFlesh uses the standard port, then, but the connecting device itself is completely nonstandard. We call it . . . "

He turned back to the chalkboard and wrote in large letters.

"We call it an UmbyCord," Witt said, and once more expressively tapped the letters. "One word, spelled like this. Capital U, capital C. Get the word right, because you're gonna be hearing a lot about UmbyCord in the months ahead."

"Based on umbilical, right?" It was someone in the front row.

"Right," said Witt. "You're getting the idea of what MetaFlesh and UmbyCord can do together. You'll also find out, like I did, that you've never tried anything quite as much fun, or anything so revolutionary, as this. Tonight, Allegra and I are going to show you some of that. This demonstration is not only free of charge, but it is *entirely without obligation to buy*. However, we're pretty confident you can all make up your own minds about that."

While they laughed again he turned with a theatrical flourish and indicated the two young assistants behind him and Allegra. They had finished laying out their weird devices on the table at the back of the platform and were now standing attentively at each end of it.

In a loud voice Witt asked, "Are the MetaFlesh Game-Pods by Antenna Research ready?"

"Yes, Mr. Levi!" said the first, and "Yes, Mr. Levi!" said the second.

"And so that these good people here tonight might try the Antenna Research MetaFlesh Game-Pods, how many of the precious prototypes did we manage to bring with us?"

"Twenty-one, Mr. Levi," said the assistant at the end of the platform closest to Pikul. She was wearing, Pikul now noticed, a worried expression on her attractive face. Clearly her answer was not the one Witt had been expecting.

His face clouded and he stepped across to the young woman.

He said in a voice that did not carry, but that Pikul was able to hear, "Only twenty-one? I thought you brought an even two dozen."

"Yes, sir," she replied softly. "But the first three we opened were . . . well, I don't know how to say it."

"Nonfunctioning?"

"More . . . unhealthy, sir."

"Are the others okay?"

"We think we're clean otherwise."

"Goddamn better be healthy," Levi snarled, but as he turned back toward the audience his face was radiant once again. "Just checking, folks!" he cried. "We have indeed twenty-one, that's one and twenty, proto-type MetaFlesh Game-Pods all ready for action here tonight. That means that for our first-wave test enclave we need one and twenty volunteers. You don't have to do much—you simply port in these slave units with the Game-Pod Goddess herself . . . "

Allegra smiled shyly at this, but already the hall was in an uproar, everyone stretching forward, reaching, pushing against the edge of the platform, imploring Witt to choose them.

Pikul took a step forward, remembering his brief to protect Allegra Geller no matter what, but he realized immediately that his entire security resources consisted of one electronic wand of untested potential and a soft plastic pink-fone.

He hoped that Wittold Levi and the assistants had the situation safely in hand. But then, he reassured himself, they must have done this sort of thing before.

[2]

For several minutes confusion reigned in the sweltering hall. The heaving mass of the audience was scrambling to get on the platform, while Pikul helped Levi and his staff fight to keep them off. The atmosphere of enthusiasm was infectious and good-natured, but beneath it there was a distinct sense of fanaticism and obsessive determination by everyone there to be the one, one of the twenty-one, who would be privileged to port into the new game with Allegra Geller.

Finally, order of a sort was restored, and Levi managed to get the crowd to group itself into four lines of more or less equal length. From these eager participants Levi and his assistants chose the privileged twenty-one by a system of random selection based on the third letter of each person's surname: the first twenty-one in alphabetical order were selected to go on the platform. Once they had worked it out, everyone accepted this system with apparent good grace, and soon most of the audience had returned to their places, and the lucky volunteers were waiting to be fitted with their game gear.

For each person, one of the assistants undid the heavy-duty snap-locks on the ski-boot plastic modules and split the case open. Inside, packed and protected in an inner case of thick Styrofoam, was the MetaFlesh Game-Pod. This looked like nothing less than a pale, living kidney, both in shape and size and the way the fleshy exterior was resilient and warm.

Coiled in the "toe" of the ski boot was the Umby-Cord for each game-pod. This was a long translucent cord, apparently filled with some kind of transparent viscous fluid. The cord was twisted and sinewy like muscle tissue, and had red and blue veinlike vessels running just beneath the surface. It was Y-shaped, with a connecting socket on each of the three ends.

As the volunteers were handed the pod and its cord, they fell into reflective silence, holding the bizarre equipment with a sense of awe and reverence. With the material in hand, each player was invited to sit in one of the twenty-two chairs placed in a semicircle facing the audience.

They were shown how to sit, and the game-pod was placed in a certain fashion on their laps. The UmbyCord was then uncoiled to its full length and one end was plugged into the port on the side of the game-pod.

The pod rippled in response.

The first time this happened, the volunteers reacted amazingly. The man on whose lap this first game-pod had been placed pushed back his chair with a scraping of its plastic legs and ripped open the front of his shirt. Half standing, holding the game-pod in place with one hand, he tried to reach behind himself with the other end of the UmbyCord and thrust the socket into the bioport that was already implanted in his back.

It was difficult for him to reach on his own, so the assistant swiftly moved in to help him.

Other people began to undo or pull their upper garments free of their waistbands.

Pikul watched all this with fascination.

A young woman sitting opposite the first man, not yet in possession of her game-pod, suddenly moaned. Her face was glowing with sweat and her hair was matted untidily around her face.

"My God!" she said in a low, aroused voice. "Oh my *God*!"

She too stood up. Her eyes were glazed. She pulled frantically at the front of her shirt, ripping the buttons apart. When she had the shirt undone, she tossed the garment to one side. She wore no bra. Her chest was already shiny with perspiration. The bioport in her back glistened expectantly, and the woman reached around to grab it, caressing it with her fingers.

She started to dribble with the passion of her sudden arousal.

A female assistant was quickly with her. She made her sit down, then retrieved the torn blouse and skillfully forced her to put it on again. The young woman continued to moan, so the assistant found a dampened cloth from somewhere and administered some cooling pressure to her forehead. Gradually, the woman volunteer calmed down.

Pikul realized that Levi and his staff must have been through this or similar situations many times before, and were prepared to deal with people's reactions to the game-pods.

He leaned forward to look at the bioport on the back of the middle-aged woman closest to him. He had only seen it in magazine photos or on TV.

The port was flesh-colored and made of soft plastic, and it was embedded somehow in the woman's back, right up against the base of her spine, just above the belt line. From more than a few inches away it was barely noticeable, resembling a faint operation scar. Close up, it could be seen as finely engineered fleshware, made to blend with the human body on which it was installed. The port itself was a small hole, about the diameter of an adult's smallest finger. As the woman shifted about in her seat, Pikul noticed that an arrangement of electronic connectors inside the bioport glittered as the bright spotlights caught them.

Gradually, Wittold Levi and his assistants imposed order. One by one the volunteers sat in the semicircle of chairs, the UmbyCord running around their waists or draped over their shoulders, and plugged into the game-pod on their laps.

Each game-pod was quivering and rippling.

When the volunteers were settled, Allegra Geller moved in to take her place in the central chair. Levi helped her with exaggerated consideration, fussing around her, seeing to her every need. Once seated with the others, Allegra clicked open her case with deliberate delicacy and removed the pod from within it.

One by one the other players connected the spare socket of their game-pods to a central prosthetic pod, thence to Allegra's own.

The Master Game-Pod. From Antenna Research.

Then Pikul was distracted.

There was a commotion of some kind close to the door and he had to wrench his attention away from Allegra and the others to see what was happening.

Someone was trying to force their way into the hall past a restraining group of men from the crowd.

Pikul squinted at the handle of his electronic wand as he hurried through the crowd, and found the On/Off switch. He turned it on. The wand hummed briefly, then continued to vibrate gently in his hand. He wasn't sure exactly what it would do, but he guessed he was about to find out.

[3]

The intruder was a man in his mid-twenties, wearing blue jeans, a white T-shirt, and a shiny leather jacket. He was carrying a large vinyl case. He was in a state of excitement, but not only was that nothing new in this unusual meeting, it might have been caused by his efforts to get past the group of men blocking his way.

"Hold it!" Pikul said loudly as he approached. He held his wand at the ready. "Not so fast. Let me see your invitation, sir."

In response, the young man thrust a card at him.

Pikul took it and tried to focus on it. It wasn't easy: it was one of those cards using a holographic ID picture, as well as validating numbers printed in machine-readable type.

"What the hell is this?" Pikul said.

"One of your invitations to this meeting, you idiot!"

"What?" Pikul looked more closely and realized that it was exactly as the young man had said. The wobbling hologram suddenly steadied, to reveal a 3-D picture of the man in front of him, as well as his name: Noel Dichter.

With his credential established, which he must have known all along it would be, Dichter was already looking anxiously past Pikul into the body of the hall. He heaved on the strap of his vinyl case, easing its weight on his shoulder.

"Oh God," he said. "I hope I'm not too late. Did I miss the port-in?"

Pikul was still trying to assess this newcomer. He seemed no different from the others already present, but exuded a nervous tension that made Pikul wary of him, and Antenna Research, he knew, considered Allegra Geller an irreplaceable asset.

"Yeah, they've started," he said. "But it's only the first wave. You can probably be part of the second wave. It's going to go on all evening." Pikul again read the name on the card. "Okay, Noel Dichter, let's see you with your arms up. I have to scan you. Metal and heavy synthetics not allowed."

"What is this?" Dichter said, incredulous. "A weapons check?"

"It's more for recording devices," Pikul said through his teeth. He was concentrating on the radio-intensity receptor control on the stem of the wand. "There's a lot of serious money invested in these games. Industrial espionage happens and, no offense, Mr. Dichter, we got to make sure it isn't going to happen here. Now, what have you got in this case?"

"I brought my game-pod," Dichter said. "It's got original Marway tissue architecture. Kind of obsolete now, I guess, but I was still hoping . . . Even though I can't afford one of your Antenna MetaFlesh 15 upgrades, I've figured out a method of virtual porting that I thought might—"

"Yeah, yeah," Pikul said, because for him not much of this made sense. "You won't need it tonight, whatever it is. Everything's provided for here by Antenna. Call it corporate hospitality."

Dichter suddenly stiffened. "My God!" he cried. "Is that who I think it is?"

"Is who who you think it is?"

"That young woman, up on the platform! Is that Allegra Geller?"

"Yeah," Pikul said, with almost paternal pride. "That's her. She's really something, isn't she?"

"What's a star like her doing here? A product launch in the back of beyond?"

"Out here in the boonies is where the real people live, you know. Real fans. Just like you, Noel."

"Yeah, well, you said it. Just like me."

Dichter had scanned clear, so with no further reason to delay him, Pikul handed his vinyl case back and waved the young man in.

Dichter went across and joined the press of people close to the platform.

Not wanting any more late arrivals to get in without his say-so, Pikul turned the lock on the door and pocketed the key. Then he wandered back to the crowd, stopping not far from Noel Dichter.

On the platform, in the center of the semicircle of linked game players, Wittold Levi finished a number of checks on the UmbyCord connectors then nodded toward Allegra Geller.

"Okay, everything seems to be in order. Are you ready, Allegra?"

She was looking pumped up, her face tense and elated, her fingers playing restlessly over the soft mound of her game-pod.

"Sure thing," she said, her voice almost singing. "This is always my favorite moment."

A wave of excited laughter passed through the crowd. Levi stepped down from the platform and went to stand amongst the audience. Allegra looked around at the other players.

"I'm about ready to start *eXistenZ* by Antenna Research," she said, her words faltering a little. She bit her lip. She went on in a much softer voice, making everyone strain forward to hear. "This will be downloaded into all of you. Let me warn you that you're in for a wild ride, but I'll be right there with you. Our assistants will be here in reality, just in case there are problems. But nothing will go wrong, because nothing can go wrong. Remember always it's just a game, a simulation. Don't panic, no matter what happens. When it's through, I'll see you all safely back here. It might seem like a long time while we're playing, but that's subjective time dilation. In reality, we will be playing for only a few minutes."

Again there was laughter, but this time it was confined to the twenty-one players on the stage. Also, it was now the nervous laughter of people uncertain of what was about to happen to them.

Allegra quickly brushed a finger over a nipplelike protuberance on the game-pod in her lap.

Immediately, the other players closed their eyes and went rigid. Their hands, resting on the pods in their laps, stiffened, and the knuckles began to show white. Meanwhile, the game-pods began a rhythmic, peristaltic rippling.

Pikul moved over to Wittold Levi.

"Allegra Geller seems shy," he said quietly. "It wouldn't have occurred to me that a big star like her would be shy."

"That's what a lot of people like about Allegra," Levi said. "She spends most of her time alone in her studio, designing the games. I sometimes think she'd be happier if she never had to show them to anybody."

"She doesn't like this adulation?"

"I don't know about that. No matter what she says

to make people feel good, it's what she's doing now that she's nervous about. Porting in with her fans. She says it's too intimate, too much of an intrusion."

"Then why does she do it?"

Levi glanced at him, grinning slyly. "I guess you could say we make her do it," he said.

"We? You mean the game company, Antenna?"

"That's what I mean."

"Why?" Pikul asked.

That look came at him again, but now Wittold Levi was no longer grinning.

"I haven't seen you before," he said, suspiciously. "Are you with Antenna, or did an independent security contractor send you?"

"I'm with you," Pikul said at once. Inwardly, he resented the man's tone, but he fished in his back pocket for his ID and showed it to Witt. "I'm working through the Antenna management training program. Security is what I'm doing right now, but I want to end up in marketing and public relations." He held up the electronic wand. "To be completely honest with you, most of what I know about security is confined to knowing how to switch this sucker on and off."

Levi ducked back from the wand, which Pikul had waved incautiously at him.

"Okay, then you'll know that corporately we've spent a fortune developing *eXistenZ*. We all realize it's a risky project. Allegra Geller might have to make more changes yet, and these kind of seminars are just about the only way we can convince her there might be a problem."

"By a problem you mean bugs?" Pikul said. "You're saying there are bugs in her new game?"

"All gameware has bugs, but we can iron them out as part of the testing and evaluation procedure. *eXistenZ* is a lot more than a game, though."

"Yeah, right. It's a game *system*. I heard you say that. It's a kind of emphasis you keep making."

"There are some top people at Antenna who are worried that *eXistenZ* is an intellectual program, too complex, too weird and artsy."

"What do you think?" Pikul asked.

"Me, I think it's the hottest product Antenna has ever had, marketwise. And Allegra's not bothered by accusations of being highbrow. Not until she faces her fans. She hates to be rejected in the flesh, so from time to time we bring her out and let her take some of the heat."

"I've heard that she's sensitive," Pikul said admiringly.

"I guess you could say that's what she's good at. We pay Allegra Geller for being sensitive."

A strange, choral humming could now be heard, filling the high vaulted roof of the old church building. Pikul and Levi turned their attention back to the stage, where the participants were rocking and swaying in their seats, moving in time with the pulsing, throbbing pods in their laps.

"What's going on now?" Pikul said quietly to Witt.

"That's the new Antenna Research theme song. We thought this might be a way to launch it. Anyone who plays *eXistenZ* is going to be familiar with that tune."

Loyally, for at heart he thought he should at least attempt to be a good company man, Pikul tried to hum along. He gave up after a few bars.

"That's catchy," he said.

Levi made no response but he too began humming, emphasizing the important notes, urging Pikul and everyone else to join in. Soon the whole room was humming along.

Everyone in the room, that is, except Noel Dichter. Pikul, never at ease with community singing, had started to glance around the room nervously, and within moments he noticed what Dichter was doing.

The young man had moved to the edge of the platform and was fumbling with the catches of his vinyl pod case. As the flap swung open, Pikul saw the fleshy mass of an old game-pod resting inside. At first he thought Dichter was going to take it out, but to his amazement he saw the man thrust his fingers straight into the resilient organic mass of the pod.

Moments later he pulled it back out, but now he was holding something small and irregularly shaped.

At first sight Pikul thought it was the half-decayed cadaver of a small animal, like a large rat or a small dog. It was made of bone and gristle and had fragments of furry flesh attached to it. Dichter used his free hand to strip away a few pieces of the gelatinous game-pod flesh still clinging to it. He held it up briefly to his eyes, checking or inspecting it.

At the front of the object was an animal's bony mouth, or snout; the little jaw was fixed open to form a rigid O. Behind this was a bulge of bony carapace, mostly blocked in by the remains of flesh or fur; Pikul could see several small bones inside, braced together like precision levers in a tiny machine. At the back, where Dichter was holding the thing, was a rigid hind leg.

Dichter held this the way he would hold the grip of a handgun. A spread of tiny foot bones formed the butt of the handle. His finger curled around a dislocated knee as if it were a trigger.

He was aiming it at Allegra Geller as he stepped up on the platform.

Pikul shouted at Wittold Levi, waving his arm wildly. "He's carrying a gun, a goddamn gun!"

Levi appeared to be blissed out, swaying as the corporate hymn surged through the air. Pikul dived away from him, launching himself through the crowd.

Dichter held the cadaver-gun in both hands and was advancing on Allegra.

"Death to *eXistenZ*!" he shouted. "Death to Antenna Research! Death to the vile demoness Allegra Geller!"

Uselessly, Pikul yelled, "Don't do it!"

He was scrambling up on to the dais as he shrieked this, and the shout succeeded in momentarily distracting Dichter. The young man glanced back to see what was happening, but instantly turned on Allegra again.

He raised the cadaver-gun.

He fired!

A loud explosion shocked everyone to silence. Allegra Geller took the full force of the bullet. She was twisted around in her chair by the impact and thrown backward to the floor. The chair spun around, landed across her and happened to be in place as Dichter fired again. This time the bullet hit the upturned underside of the chair and was deflected away from her. It zinged through the air and ricocheted from an overhead lamp shade.

As Allegra fell, the neural surge communicated itself to the other players hooked into her game-pod.

They all gasped, thrust their heads back, swayed back and forth perilously on their chairs.

Allegra was still conscious, but was sprawling painfully on the hard surface of the platform. The bullet had buried itself in her shoulder. She pressed her good hand against it, trying to ease the pain. Otherwise she lay still, watching in terror through half-opened eyes. She was breathing harshly, letting out whimpers of pain.

On their chairs, twenty-one other players clutched their shoulders.

Pikul's dash across the stage was completed as he launched himself into a flying tackle. He brought Dichter crashing to the floor. Dichter fired twice more as they fell together, hitting the two participants closest to Allegra. Both flew backward from their chairs and fell to the wooden floor.

Pikul used his security wand at last, repeatedly whacking Dichter across the face, neck, and arms. Each blow induced a galvanic convulsion of pain in the man, but he was not disabled. Struggling to get away from Pikul, he managed to bring his gun hand around.

Pikul found himself staring into the open O of an animal's snout, where smoke still lingered.

He threw himself backward to escape, and Dichter managed at last to scramble to his knees.

Wittold Levi and his assistants had by now run back onto the stage and were dashing across toward Dichter. The young attacker saw them coming and swung the cadaver-gun around.

He caught Wittold Levi full in the chest. As the bullet struck him, the man fell backward and crashed painfully to the stage floor amongst the jumble of overturned chairs, fallen game-pods and writhing UmbyCords.

The female assistant Pikul had noticed earlier pulled a conventional pistol from a shoulder harness beneath her jacket. She steadied her gun hand, took careful aim, then fired two calm and accurate shots into the side of Dichter's head. He crumpled immediately, amid a spurting fountain of cranial blood.

The chaos did not end here, because the game players were quickly reemerging from their participation in the game. Blasted by the psychic waves of pain from Allegra, they were in full panicky urge to escape.

Everyone jostled, pushed, and screamed, trying to get away from the confusion, the dramatic slashes of spilled blood and the tangle of fallen bodies on the platform. Meanwhile, friends and relatives who had been watching from the audience were trying to climb up to the platform to help.

As he clambered to his feet, Pikul was clouted from behind by a game-pod swinging on the end of its UmbyCord; the soft and surprisingly massy weight knocked him full-length. He sprawled across someone. Muttering automatic apologies, he tried to get to his feet.

The man turned desperately to face him. It

was Wittold Levi, his face contorted with agony.

"Get her out of here, Pikul!" he said fiercely. His voice was a gasping parody of the smooth tones he had spoken in before. "Save her! That man's not acting alone! There are probably more of them out there somewhere!"

"Save who?" Pikul said stupidly.

"Allegra Geller! Get her away from this place. Do it now!"

"Me?" said Pikul.

"Trust no one." Levi's eyes were glazing, and his voice was weaker. "Trust no one. There are enemies everywhere. Out there, in here . . . everywhere. Even in our own house! The corporation cannot protect—"

Levi made an appalling belching, vomiting sound and his face turned darkly purple. His eyes closed and his body convulsed again.

Pikul backed away, twisting around to find Allegra. As he did, he tripped again, and this time sprawled across Dichter's body. Full of horror he levered himself up, pressing down on something hard and springy beneath his hand.

When he finally regained his feet, he discovered he was holding Dichter's cadaver-gun.

Levi's assistants were approaching him, both carrying weapons at the ready. Without thinking twice, Pikul shoved the cadaver-gun deep into his trouser pocket, forcing it in, feeling it bend and yield. Like supple muscle tissue.

There was no sign of Allegra.

Standing there, still foolishly clutching his electronic wand, Pikul looked around desperately for her.

He saw the prosthetic junction pod where all the UmbyCords had met to join Allegra's master pod. It was lying on the floor with an UmbyCord stretching out and over the edge of the stage. When he looked, Allegra was down there, twisted painfully in the angle between the main hall floor and the raised section of the platform.

He leaped down to her.

He established two things with great speed: that she was still alive, and that she was suffering considerable pain.

Where the tautly stretched UmbyCord was connected to her, it was wrenching on the bioport on the lower part of her back. With great presence of mind, Pikul slipped his hand underneath the tight fabric of her T-shirt and managed to release the connector from the port.

As the connector slipped out she slumped forward and her body relaxed. She groaned loudly, then with blind movements managed to get herself upright. With Pikul's assistance she regained her feet and stood close to him, swaying slightly.

Two of her fans approached, trying to push Pikul

aside to get to her. He forced them back with a vicious swing of the wand.

"Stay away from her!" he shouted. "Allegra's coming with me! I'm taking charge of her!"

The fans backed off, and next to him Allegra stirred. Amazingly, she laughed weakly.

"I'm coming with *you?*" she said incredulously.

"Yeah, lady," Pikul said. "You're with me from now on. Until I get further orders from Antenna."

Although she was clutching the bloodied wound in her shoulder and looked extremely dazed, Allegra Geller appeared to be rational and capable of movement. Pikul put his hand under the elbow of her good arm and helped to swing her around. The moment she regained her balance, she unexpectedly turned away from him and scrambled back up on the platform.

"I can't lose my pod!" she shouted, above the racket of the panicking voices still swelling around them.

Her pod had fallen under one of the overturned chairs. She hurried across and grabbed it, pausing for a couple of seconds to examine it. Her gestures, her body language, reminded Pikul of a mother with a small baby. Apparently satisfied that the pod was undamaged, she looked around for her pod case and managed to retrieve it from the edge of the platform. She slid the game-pod and its UmbyCord inside and snapped the lid closed.

Pikul dashed across to her, took her hand and hauled her through the crowd.

In spite of everything that had just happened, people recognized her as the star and turned to her, trying to reach out and touch her.

Pikul barged his way through, holding the electronic wand menacingly before him.

The main door was locked. Pikul groaned inwardly. He now remembered locking it himself, to keep out more people like Dichter, but the key was somewhere deep in his pocket, with a gun made out of a dead animal's body pushed in tightly on top of it. He had neither time nor inclination to go hunting around for the key. They had to move immediately. He silently congratulated himself bitterly on his own lousy planning.

"Over there!" Allegra shouted to him. "At the side."

It looked like a door that wouldn't take them outside, but when Pikul kicked it open, they found themselves in a short corridor leading to a kitchen. On the far side of the room was another door. It sprang open with the help of Pikul's boot, and moments later they were outside in the calm, scented air. Cicadas rasped in the placid nighttime heat. Stars shone with reassuring normality overhead.

"Does that happen everywhere you go?" he said to Allegra, panting with sudden exhaustion.

She simply shook her head, clutching her injured shoulder. Pikul glanced back through a window at the illuminated interior of the hall. He could see part of the platform. Five or six of the fans had found Dichter's body and were kicking it in a frenzy of hatred and revenge. Wittold Levi's two assistants were carrying away Levi's body with great care and tenderness.

"Come on, lady," Pikul said. "Time to be out of here."

[4]

They emerged from the church hall at the side. Pikul rushed her along the path to the front. The parking lot he'd been in earlier was here, reaching as far as the edge of the highway and around to the other side of the building. He dragged her along, heading past the main door.

"Where are we going?" she shouted.

"To my car. I parked it on the other side."

"No . . . forget that. We'll take my limo." She pointed to the Land Rover Defender.

"No way!" Pikul said.

"Why not? What's the problem?"

"I don't trust the driver."

"Who? Frances? *You* can drive, you idiot!"

They hurried across to the Defender and Pikul pulled open the passenger door. Frances, a magazine propped up on the dash under the dome light, looked startled at their sudden arrival.

"You again?" she said.

"Start the engine, ma'am. We got to go."

"I don't take orders from you, young man!"

"Frances?" Allegra's voice rose up from behind Pikul. "We need the car."

"What's all the commotion, Miss Geller?"

"No commotion. We have to leave."

Frances noticed Allegra's blood-soaked sleeve.

"Are you all right, Miss Geller?" she said anxiously. "What's been going on back there?"

"Things got a little out of hand. But now we'd like to be on our way. I guess I must tell you we need this vehicle, and we need it with the keys. But this time we want it without you."

"Miss Geller, you know I drive for you, but my paycheck comes from Antenna. I can't abandon my vehicle without the say-so of my boss."

Allegra moved swiftly, stretching her good hand around Pikul's back and slipping her hand brusquely into his trouser pocket. He jumped in astonishment at the intimacy the feeling gave him. When she withdrew her hand, she was holding the cadaver-gun. She pointed it at Frances's face.

"Get down from the driver's seat, Frances," Allegra said. "You can tell your boss you were hijacked."

"Sorry, Miss Geller," Frances said, and chuckled. "It's gonna take more than a dead squirrel to get me out of this seat."

Pikul was going to explain about the gun but Allegra wasted no more time. She fired two shots, the first through the side window behind Frances's head, the second into the cushion of the headrest.

"Shit!" Pikul shouted, his head ringing from the explosions.

Frances was already halfway out of the car.

"You have to push down the shift lever to get it into reverse," she said at the window. "It's got a nearly full tank of gas. Don't use four-wheel drive unless you need to."

Her head dropped down out of sight.

"Thanks, Frances," Allegra called.

Pikul moved across into the driver's seat, and Allegra followed him into the vehicle, slamming the door behind her.

Pikul turned the ignition, and the engine fired smoothly right away. They lowered both windows to vent the gun smoke out. Pikul was momentarily confounded by the unfamiliar manual gear lever and the reach of the pedals, but he'd driven many different kinds of vehicles in the past. He swung the heavy Land Rover around in reverse, then bumped and crashed across the verge and made a lurching turn onto the highway. He put his foot to the floor and they accelerated away.

They headed north, toward the distant line of mountains.

↔   ↔   ↔

The cones of the headlights picked out the road ahead. The white division markings in the center of the highway shot soundlessly by beneath their wheels, like tracer shells fired low from far ahead. The engine made a powerful, soothing sound, and the interior of the saloon was lined with thick, noise-suppressing fabric, but the hard suspension transmitted the uneven surface of the road to them.

Allegra was wedged against the door stanchion, her head tipped away from him, her face pale in the glow from the dash. After their getaway had been secured and they were certain no other vehicle was in pursuit, she'd lapsed into this withdrawn state. Her hands rested listlessly in her lap, and she responded to his questions with vague movements of her head. Pikul had given up trying to talk to her after a few minutes, and let the road sweep by and the miles build up.

Finally, she stirred, focusing on the restricted nighttime view ahead. A semi, its headlights undipped and glaring at them, approached on the other side, a curve of orange glitter-lights surrounding the cab. They'd barely registered this when the thing thundered past and out of sight. The Land Rover shook in the wash of turbulent air that followed the truck's passage. Allegra peered through the window at her side: vague shapes of trees and open land could be glimpsed under the moon.

"We'll drive out of this farmland," she said, her voice sounding none too strong. "There's sure to be a junction on the highway soon. Whichever way there's a turn, take it. We'll drive for a while, find a safe place to stop."

She shifted awkwardly in the seat, changing position.

Pikul glanced across at her, suddenly contrite.

"I'd almost forgotten—you've been shot. How are you feeling?"

She turned away from him again. "It's stopped bleeding," she said quietly, "and it isn't hurting as much. It's gone all numb. I can hold on for a while. But I guess you're right: I've been shot."

"I've never been near anyone being shot before," Pikul said.

"Me neither."

"I kind of thought . . . "

"What?"

"Well, you know, needing a security guard. Normal people don't have a security guard."

"Normal people don't get fired at by maniacs holding dead animals."

"That's kind of what I'm saying. Sorry." He stared ahead at the uncertain destination. "You know, about being shot . . . it was almost as if you were expecting it."

"I expect you to get me home safely. That's all."

"All right."

The vehicle lurched wildly again.

He noticed that she was still gripping the injured shoulder with her free hand. The rolling motion of the Rover must have been agony for her, whatever she said.

After a few more minutes the vehicle rose slightly and they crossed a smoother stretch of road. Girders flashed by on both sides, and they saw a glimpse of a broad river silver in the night. Then they were back on the regular highway surface, lurching on the ill-maintained blacktop. There had been a turnoff just past the bridge. Pikul slowed the vehicle to walking speed, then wheeled it around in a U-turn in the dark. He headed back. Moments later they saw the bridge again, and Pikul turned the Land Rover through the small intersection. Driving slowly again, running alongside the river, he followed the narrow road through a swathe of overhanging trees. Insects hovered brightly in the beams of their headlights. Soon the road turned toward the north, climbing through wilder country. When they came out from the trees there was no more sign of the river. The mountains were ahead of them, much closer now.

"Have you any idea where we are?" he said to her.

"Not now. Keep going. This must lead somewhere into the mountains. That's okay, because I know places we could go."

The Land Rover's movements were suddenly much easier to live with.

Several minutes later, Pikul said reflectively, "I normally like the countryside, don't you? It's usually relaxing and calm."

"That's only if you don't know what's going on."

"What do you mean?"

"There is great stress and anger and violence in the countryside," Allegra said, with unexpected vehemence. She'd swiveled in her seat to stare across at him. For a moment he thought she was going to do something inexplicable and violent against him; there was a sense of darkness and mystery in her that was not wholly explained by the wound she had suffered. He glanced back at the road, then at her. "There are thousands of life-forms everywhere in the countryside," she went on. "All screaming *me! me! me!* and trying to kill and dominate and devour the other life-forms. It's a terrifying and exhausting place!"

She fell silent, looking out into the dark night.

"Well, I like the countryside," Pikul said lamely.

"That's good. Because I reckon you might end up spending a lot of time out here."

"I might?"

"Sure. If you go back home to the city, they'll be waiting for you."

"They?"

"Yeah. My assassins. The ones you thwarted.

They'll probably want to have a little talk with you about where I am."

Pikul thought about that for a moment. "Don't you think," he said, "that might have been just one crazy guy acting alone?"

"Didn't you hear the way he screamed at me? He wasn't alone. He had been sent."

"Sent," Pikul said. "Out to a rural town, on the chance you might be there."

"You don't know anything about this business I'm in."

"I'm learning fast. You mean all that? That there's a group of people out for your head?"

"How would you explain what happened back there?"

"Everybody likes a conspiracy," Pikul said. "It's more satisfying than just one crazy guy doing one crazy thing."

"Suit yourself."

She turned away again. He sneaked another look at her and saw, in the light from the dash, that she was biting her lower lip. She still gripped her injured shoulder.

They drove into the deepening night. The only sign of habitation was the occasional glimpse of a light from a house or a window, flickering beyond trees. Every now and again Allegra would turn stiffly in her seat to look back, to see if anything might be following them. Nothing ever was. Just the road ahead in the headlight beams, the road behind in the dark, the trees and the undulating hill country.

"Well, what's next?" Pikul said in a while. "What are we going to do out here? Do you know your way around? Do you know any country people?"

"Not country people," she said. "But I know games people, and most of them are out here. The countryside's scattered with games development people, project coordinators, little assembly factories . . . you name it."

"That's weird. I never knew that."

She gave him a look that he caught by chance, turning toward her briefly as he drove. The look told him he never knew anything.

"Cities are full of bad microwaves, bad thermals, bad electrooptics, digital networks, FM transmitters, bleepers, radar alarm devices. There's so much of that shit you can't shield it out anymore. Readings aren't true. The whole industry moved out of the city years ago."

"Silicon Valley, and all that?"

"No. That's still the city. I'm talking about farms, small holdings, houses in valleys, places where crowds and traffic don't go. That's the future, you know. The industrial revolution brought people into the cities, and the electronics revolution, the *systems* revolution, is taking them out again."

"So you can find your way around."

"Some."

"Where are we heading at the moment?"

"I don't know about you, but I'm going to need somewhere to stay tonight. That's a start."

"Do you have somewhere in mind?"

"Not immediately. Tomorrow, perhaps."

"But there are places you know where we can hide out?" he said.

"Maybe . . . but I'm discovering I have some enemies I didn't know I had. 'Death to Allegra Geller!' How'd you like to hear somebody coming at you with a gun screaming your name at you?"

"Wow," Pikul said, thinking about that.

"'Death to Ted Pickle' . . . pretty scary, huh?"

"It's Pikul, not Pickle. Anyway, how'd you—"

"It says 'Pickle' on your name badge."

"I don't pronounce it that way."

"Okay, I'm sorry. You can drop the Allegra and call me Geller. Almost everyone else does, the ones who know me. I like that, never been comfortable with my given name."

"All right . . . Geller."

"That's fine, Pikul. Now we're friends."

He thought about that too, and decided he liked it. He just wished she'd act like a friend. She seemed to have an attractive personality, what little he'd seen of it in the church, but toward him she exuded suspicion, fear, belief that he was part of the conspiracy against her.

"That gun the guy brought with him," he said. "How did you know how to fire it? I've never seen anything like it before."

"It has a trigger," she replied casually. "I guessed it was meant to be pulled, so I pulled it."

"May I see it?"

"Later. You know, I'm thinking I might use it in my next game."

A pothole appeared unexpectedly, and the Land Rover lurched and bounced. He heard Geller gasping, and saw that the stain of blood had spread further while they'd been talking.

"You're bleeding again," he said. "I keep forgetting you got hit. You don't talk like someone dying of gunshot wounds."

"I might start dying of gunshot wounds if we don't do something about it soon."

Something large and insectlike buzzed against Pikul's chest, and he reflexively jerked a flapping hand at it. Then he remembered what it was. While steering with one hand he pulled the pink-fone out of his shirt pocket.

"What's that?" Geller said.

"My pink-fone. Head office. I'm not sure I should answer it."

"Answer it," she said.

He squelched the soft sides, and the diffused pink internal light swelled up once more.

"Yeah . . . Pikul." He heard the hiss of digital zoning. Then somewhere in the distance, like a pop of compressed air, the line cleared. The voice that spoke was deep and close, as if it were coming from the rear of the vehicle they were in.

"Pikul, what in hell's happened?"

"Some fan went crazy, sir. He started shooting up the place. No one knows why. Maybe he was just nuts."

"Maybe he was out for the bounty," said the voice. "There's five million dollars on Allegra Geller's head. A fringe group calling themselves the 'Anti-eXistenZial-ists' have put up the price. It's been on TV tonight, and it'll be on every newspaper front page tomorrow morning. That's the kind of crazy nut he was. Anyway, what happened to Geller? The information I have is that she survived, but is she safe?"

"Yeah."

"Where is she?"

"She's with me now. I'm taking care of her."

"What do you mean she's with you? Where exactly are you?"

"Well, we still can't be too far from where the meeting was. We're in the car heading north, and we've been driving fast for maybe half an hour, so I guess by now we must be—"

Pikul never completed the sentence, because without warning Geller reached across and grabbed the pink-fone from him. She fumbled around with it a moment, trying to find a way of turning it off. She must have pressed some other key, because the instrument suddenly screeched and a curl of printout paper shot through a slot in the top. Geller ripped this off then stared at it in the glow from the dash.

She looked up sharply at Pikul.

The voice of the man Pikul had been speaking to continued to sound from the headset.

"Geller, let me have my pink-fone back."

"Shit to that, Pikul!"

She fiddled with it again, this time managing to turn the power off. The pink light faded.

She put her arm out through the open window and tossed the fone as far away from the Rover as she could.

"Hey, what the hell did you do that for?" Pikul said, shocked by the suddenness of her action. "That was our lifeline to civilization."

"That was civilization's lifeline to us, Pikul. It contains a satellite-sensitive rangefinder. So long as we carry the pink-fone, they'll know where we are to within about five yards."

"They? You mean at Antenna, at the head office?"

"I mean anybody with the right technology. Look, I heard what Wittold Levi said to you, back there at the meeting. He said we have enemies in our own house. He said it as he was dying."

The vehicle swerved as Pikul took in the significance of this unwelcome reminder.

"I don't think Levi *died*," he said, disturbed by the idea. "You know, I mean . . . really dead. Do you? I think maybe he fainted, went unconscious. Quite a lot unconscious, if you like, but not really, totally *dead*."

She gestured impatiently. "Who was that on the phone, Pikul? What was he saying to you?"

"It was Mr. Kindred."

"Alex Kindred? Head of PR and marketing?"

"Right. Alex Kindred, on that highly expensive pink-fone you threw away."

"What was he saying?"

"He said there was a group who've put up a bounty. Five million dollars—"

"Yeah, the Anti-eXistenZialists. I heard about them on the car radio when we were driving over this evening. The games world is full of crazy people."

"These sound like *dangerous* crazy people. If that guy Dichter is anything to go on—"

"I guess he was one of them."

"But what do they have against you?"

She shuddered. "Maybe you'd have to ask them. They've never exactly sat down with me and argued it out. But I don't think it's personal. You know, against me in person. I created *eXistenZ* and they're pretty unhappy about that. They say it's a game system that will finally destroy reality."

"Will it?"

"It's just a game, Pikul."

"But will it?"

"No, of course not."

He stared straight ahead, seeing the dark road leading them on through the anonymous countryside. He wished they would come to a town or a signpost so he could find out where they were. Ahead there was only darkness, without even a hint of habitation.

"This all makes sense to you?" he asked her. "You don't seem surprised about any of it."

"I hear things. It's hard to surprise me with anything. People in the game world are mostly okay, but there are a few crazies. You always get crazies, no matter what you do. What else did Kindred say?"

"Not a lot more. If you remember, you took away the pink-fone before we could finish. I think he sees me as your bodyguard, and that the Antenna Corporation is holding me responsible for your safety."

"A bodyguard, you say?"

"I do what I can," Pikul said modestly.

"Where do you keep your gun, bodyguard?"

"What?"

"Your gun. Bodyguards carry guns."

"I'm one of the new generation of bodyguards. We have secret techniques."

"You're bullshitting. I know you aren't armed. You didn't even know what to do with the dead rat. How can you protect me without weapons?"

"I've got an electronic wand."

"You mean your Boy Scout cattle prod? More like a calf prod for geeks! Get serious, Pikul."

Bristling, he said, "Look, Geller, I'll do what I can to save your life, but you ought to know I'm only a marketing trainee. My clinic master said I had to know how the whole company worked, so tonight he got me to moonlight as a security guard on your test preview."

"That's great, isn't it?" Geller said. "Fucking great. I'm marked for death and they send me out on the road with a PR nerd."

She stared angrily out of her side window. He reached out a hand to try to reassure her, but the moment his fingers brushed against her arm, she snatched it away from him. Then she let out a yell as the motion jerked her injured shoulder. Still she stared away from him, out into the night.

Pikul felt himself rising defensively to respond, but then thought better of it. He subsided mentally and for a few minutes concentrated on driving, but the larger implications of all this were starting to crowd in on him.

"You really are marked for death, aren't you?" he said after a while. "Do you know what you did?"

"Yeah."

"Don't you think I have a right to know too?"

"Don't sweat about it, Pikul. I can handle it. All we have to do is disappear for a while, and I reckon even you can do that without bungling it."

"Thanks."

"Meanwhile, we have to stop."

"What, here?"

"Right now. Stop the car, please. Over there on the side."

"Why?"

Geller said, through gritted teeth, "It's time you and I had an intimate moment alone together."

[5]

The intimate moment alone together occurred in the middle of the narrow road, between the trees. Insects stridulated in the warm summer night around them. Overhead, the leaves and branches were still and silent, casting the road into moonless shadows. They left the Land Rover with its engine idling, and went around to the front, into the full glare of the head-lights. Geller kneeled down on the hard tarmac, removed her jacket, and pulled the loose neck of her T-shirt down to bare her injured shoulder.

Pikul, full of squeamishness and painfully aware of his total lack of experience, went about digging out the bullet with his Swiss Army knife. He tried to do it slowly, he tried to do it gently. But what he actually did was do it slowly.

Her eyes bright with tears, Geller said, "C'mon, Pikul, *c'mon!* If you're gonna do it, do it!"

"I don't want to hurt you."

"You failed. You're hurting me. Just get the goddamn bullet out of me before I pass out."

"Don't faint," he pleaded.

"All right, I'm not about to faint. But I am likely to kill if you don't finish up soon."

"Okay, okay. I'm doing my best."

Sweat was bursting from his brow. He clenched his teeth and dug into the wound more recklessly than before. He could feel something hard and rounded inside, something that resisted the sharp point of the knife blade. If he could get the point a little deeper, to the side . . .

Something yellow and white flipped out of the wound and shot in a glistening arc through the brilliant beams from the headlights.

Geller gasped with agony and ducked away from him, once more clamping her hand over the aching, bleeding injury. She hung her head with her hair hiding her face, her breath rasping in and out.

Pikul dropped the knife and shuffled across to where he'd seen the object fall. He soon found it, lying on the tarmac surface of the road. It was hard and slippery, and eluded his grasp the first time he tried to pick it up. He wiped it with his fingers, then took it back to her, holding it up in the light.

"I got it. Look at that!"

"You found the bullet. Big deal."

"No, look! Did someone bite you?"

"What do you mean?" Geller said, turning toward him. Her face was drawn and pale with pain.

"What I just dug out of you. It's a tooth. A human tooth."

He held it out for her to see, but after a quick glance. Geller turned away. She leaned back into the dark, found her MetaFlesh game-pod bag and rummaged around inside it.

"Let's take another look at that weirdo pistol," she said.

She quickly located the cadaver-gun and held it in both hands, examining it from different angles. After a moment of expert study she found the magazine, and popped it out of the grip. She examined it in the harsh light of the headlights, then passed it to Pikul.

The magazine, made of sheets of bone and fragments of gristle, was packed with teeth.

"What in hell . . . ?" Pikul said.

"As you said, the bullets are human teeth." She held them close to her eyes and looked intently at them. "Look, this one's got a cavity."

"Filled with amalgam?" Pikul said, trying to make the gun normal in some horrid way.

"No, there's no amalgam," she said seriously. "That's a metal compound, isn't it? An alloy of mercury and silver?"

"I got it!" Pikul said, trying to grab the cadaver-gun from her. She kept it away from him. "No metal anywhere in the whole damn thing," he said. "That gun is designed to go through metal or synthetics detectors. The whole thing is made of flesh and bone. Dichter got past me with that! I screened him with my wand, and there was no metal anywhere on him."

"I guess you're right."

"Sure I'm right. It's incredible they'd go to so much trouble."

Geller was looking giddy with disbelief about their bizarre discovery. "If they made smaller-caliber weapons," she said, "they'd have to fill them with baby teeth! The tooth fairy could go into the arms business!"

"Dichter really did intend to kill you tonight."

Geller looked at him long and hard, until Pikul found her gaze unnerving and had to look away. She remained silent. When he looked back, she was still staring at him, deep in thought.

"Yeah, I think he did," Geller said soberly, returning from her brief flight of fantasy.

[6]

They stopped off at a Perky Pat to buy some take-out burgers, then rented a room at a place called the Salmon Falls Motel. The ill-lit room was furnished with old, dark wallpaper, a grimy carpet that once had been colored orange, and two large double beds. They each sat on one of the beds, putting the paper bags and food containers on the floor between them. They ate hungrily, dropping pieces of salad and gobbets of relish on the floor.

Neither of them said anything. Pikul was thinking about the rest of the night and having to share a bedroom with a woman who looked and acted the way Allegra Geller did. Even tired, injured, and frightened as she undoubtedly was, she acted casual, often affording him quick little smiles he found tantalizing and enthralling. He couldn't figure her out, though. She wasn't leading him on: nothing in anything she said or did gave that impression. She was just . . . good to be with. She seemed relaxed and familiar in his company, taking him for granted. At the motel office he'd asked for two separate rooms, but Geller intervened and told the clerk they wanted only one room.

"You bodyguard," she'd said by way of explanation, as they headed down to find the room. "Me potential victim. Like it or not, you don't leave my side tonight."

Pikul had come to the conclusion he could put up with the situation.

As soon as she was through eating, Geller went into the bathroom and turned on the shower. She pushed the door behind her, but neither locked nor closed it properly. The sound of rushing and splashing water drifted sensuously into the room. Pikul sat quietly on his bed, picking at his teeth with a fingernail and thinking about the most beautiful woman he'd ever met, naked and wet only a few feet away from him. Practically in the same room with him.

Then, a few minutes later, she *was* in the same room with him, her legs and shoulders still glistening with droplets. Allegra had wound a damp, inadequate motel towel around her body, and wrapped an even smaller one about her hair. She paced restlessly around the room for a while, dabbing the water off herself. Her thoughts were obviously miles away.

The towel was thin and threadbare from years of use, and clung to her body revealingly. To Pikul, she was a vision of naked arms and legs, and temptingly hinted at curves, at which he hardly dare glance.

The wound in her shoulder was still exposed, but it had stopped bleeding and the hot water had helped clean it up a little. At her suggestion, Pikul went out to the Land Rover and found the small onboard first-aid kit. He helped her place a dressing on the wound: an antiseptic lint pad held in place by two large plasters.

The physical nearness of her dazzled him; she smelled wonderfully of soap and shampoo. Water dripped from her hair onto his knee. As he placed the dressing on her shoulder she inclined her face, and he almost went mad at the shapes she made: the cool angles of collarbone, neck, throat, cheek, lips, soft skin, fair hair, gentle womanhood.

Afterward, he cleaned up the mess they had made with the food, while Geller sat across from him in the middle of the other bed. She had placed her game-pod on the towel covering her lap and jacked the Umby-Cord into the bioport in her back. Her eyes were closed and her fingers twitched delicately over the sensitive surface of the game-pod. She seemed to be in a kind of trance, her body moving voluptuously in time to some unheard rhythm.

Pikul stared, entranced by the stresses her movements were causing on the too-small towel that so inadequately covered her body. The knot she'd tied in the towel under her armpit was working loose, as he'd secretly hoped all along it might. He watched with close interest as the edge of the piece of cloth slipped with maddening slowness, millimeter by millimeter, down the curve of her left breast. He was torn with indecision: Should he be the perfect gentleman and look away? Should he gently cover her? Or should he instead pretend not to notice, and let gravity and nature take their course?

Before he had to decide, Geller suddenly came out of her trance. She opened her eyes, saw him there and leaned over her pod to make some final adjustment. As she did, two things happened at once: the towel finally worked completely loose and her hand came up and grabbed it just in time.

She stared hard at the game-pod while she retied the knot under her arm.

When she spoke, it was in vague terms, not directly addressing him.

"The whole game world is in a kind of trance," she said.

"I remember you said something like that, back at the meeting." He realized his voice sounded a tone or two higher than usual.

"People are willing to accept so little," she said. "They habitually sell themselves short. They're trapped in a cage formed out of their own limited expectations. They think that what they see is everything they know, or everything they can ever know. They won't imagine or dream or fantasize. To most people the limit of their horizon is a vacation every year, a trip away from home. Some people don't even do as much as that. Yet the whole world is out there, waiting to be discovered. But now there's more than just the world: virtual reality adds an extra dimension. You can explore the whole world, more than the whole world, simply by using your mind. The problem is a kind of courage. You need courage to throw off everything that's familiar, to experiment. Very few people can conceive the amazing experiences that could be theirs were they only more daring."

She stared reflectively at the dark wallpaper opposite the beds. Part of it was peeling, to reveal dark plaster beneath. She seemed untroubled by their dingy surroundings, wrapped up in her own thoughts.

Pikul said, "Just now with your game-pod . . . where were you? What were you doing?"

"I was wandering through *eXistenZ* . . . the new system, I mean."

"Yeah. I could see that. But what were you actually doing?"

She looked directly at him, and for a moment he could have sworn he saw her tongue flick with quick relish across her lips. Then she smiled shyly and glanced away from him.

"Wandering," she said. "I told you. That's about all I can do on my own, all anyone can do. It's kind of interesting, but only in the way a foreign country is interesting to a tourist. I was trapped in the cage of my own making. To get really involved you have to react to another player. It's the old saying: it takes two. It can get pretty frustrating on your own."

As she finished saying this she looked directly into his eyes, and the invitation was unmistakable.

"Would you like to play with me?" she asked. She turned toward him, her hand indicating the game-pod.

"Me?" he said. "But I've never . . . " Pikul felt panic inexplicably rising in him. Everything in him urged him to keep her at a distance. "Let's get this problem sorted out!" he said, allowing the words to run out of him uncontrollably. "Why won't you let me contact Antenna? They'll be going crazy wondering what's happened to you. I mean, it's not like we've done anything wrong. We just ran because we didn't know how many of them there were. Right? I think we owe it to Antenna to let them know you're all right, to get them to send somebody to help you who knows what he's doing . . . "

As he said all this Geller was unbuttoning his shirt, while continuing to stare invitingly into his eyes. When the last button was undone, she gently pulled the flaps out from his trousers and ran her arms around his waist. The tips of her breasts pressed softly through her thin towel against his bare chest, and he could smell her still-damp hair.

He stopped speaking, and waited for heaven to erupt around him.

Then she said, stepping back from him, "Where's your bioport?"

"My bioport?" he said stupidly.

"Don't tell me you were never fitted!"

"I was never fitted. Who cares?"

"You work for Antenna Research and you don't have a bioport? It's incredible. You've never played one of my games because you've never played *any* game."

"Look, Allegra—I mean Geller—I'm on this management training program, and my clinic master—"

"Fuck your clinic master! This is about me, not some goddamn careerist at Antenna. It means you've no idea what a genius I am."

"A genius, huh?" Pikul wanted her to put her arms around him again, but she had backed right off. "I don't need to play a game to know how to sell it."

"That's Antenna talking. It's bullshit, posturing bullshit. If you don't play my games, you aren't going to work for Antenna. I can make sure of that."

"Look, I've been dying to play your games," Pikul said, not entirely truthfully. "But I have this . . . phobia. A phobia about having my body penetrated."

"Oh yeah?"

"Penetrated surgically, I mean. You understand, don't you?"

"I'm not so sure I do. Getting penetrated is the dream of most of the girls I know."

"In case you haven't noticed, I'm not a girl." Pikul realized this relationship was grinding to a halt even before it had begun. He knew he'd fallen into a hole and was busy digging it deeper. He decided to try shifting ground, giving way a little. "Maybe a bioport would be different, though?"

"It's different."

"I dunno . . . I need to be talked into it. I can't do it. It's too freaky. Makes my skin crawl."

"For God's sake, Pikul. Come on . . . they just pop something against your spine with a little hydrogun. Shoot the port plug into it. They do it at malls, like getting your ears pierced."

Pikul winced. Ear piercing was something else he had a phobia about.

"You saw those people at the meeting," Geller went on. "They've all had ports fitted. Farmers, delivery drivers, kids at college, senior citizens, cops, you name it. Millions of people have fitted bioports. It's just a quick jab."

"Yeah, sure. With only an infinitesimal chance of permanent spine paralysis. I read about that in the *National Enquirer.*"

"You chose this profession, geek."

"Can't you talk me into it?" Pikul said, thinking she hadn't really tried that hard yet.

"You mean other than logically?"

"Yeah . . . what's the best thing about it? Illogically?"

That obviously touched something in her. "You like intimacy with someone else?" she said. "You like to get real close? You like to feel and hold and have someone?"

"Sure I do."

"There's nothing closer than two people together in *eXistenZ*." She stepped back to him again, tipping her appealing face up toward his. She came up close; not touching, but so near he could feel her breath moving lightly across the skin of his chest. "When you play *eXistenZ* with someone else, you feel there's an intimacy that is beyond expression. You'll never have experienced anything like it in your real life, because you can't get that close in real life. Wouldn't you like to try? You can play all sorts of games with me if you like."

He was swirling with emotions and confusion. When she said games, did she mean . . . ? He'd like to play with her, of course, but were they thinking about the same thing?

"That's what I thought you—" he started. "When you . . . you know, when you undid my shirt—"

"I was looking for your bioport."

"Yes, I know that *now*, but at the time."

"You thought I wanted something else. Maybe I did, maybe I didn't. Listen, once we've ported together there are no limits on what we can play. No rules, no inhibitions. I'm asking you if you'll play *eXistenZ* with me."

"You want to do it now?"

"Sure. But you know why not?"

"Because . . . because I don't have a bioport."

"That's right. You don't have a bioport."

Now he backed away from her. She was making him sweat, and he didn't want her to see how much. He made a play of needing to get his shirt back on, then got the buttons mixed up and had to turn his back on her while he sorted that out. He deliberately didn't think about what she seemed to be offering him: she was so *available*, yet he could not have her.

When he looked back at her, she'd sat down on the edge of the bed once more, cradling her pod on her lap.

"You going to go back into the game now?" Pikul asked.

"No. Come and see this." He moved across to her. "My baby took a huge hit back there, at the meeting. You see how she's quivering?"

He peered down at the pod. It was indeed shivering, with tight peristaltic convulsions rippling through the body.

He said, "Yes, it . . . I mean she is quivering."

"I'm not just being sentimental, Pikul. This baby is the most highly developed piece of organware in the world. When those UmbyCords were ripped out of her, back at the church, it was at the most vulnerable time for her. The game architecture was being downloaded from her to the slave pods. The software protocols that achieve that are some of the most sophisticated that game architecture has ever seen. God knows what damage that might have caused. Do you see the problem?"

"Well, I—"

"The only way I can tell if everything's okay, can be sure the game hasn't been contaminated, is for me to play *eXistenZ* with someone I trust. Someone friendly." She looked up at him again. Her lips were glistening and her eyes had a gleam of danger in them. "You say I can trust you, but are you friendly?"

"Yeah, I'm friendly. Look at me. Completely friendly."

"But you don't have a bioport."

"I'll get one," Pikul said. "It can't be too difficult if all those delivery boys, farmers, those people you said, if they've got them. Okay, we're miles out in the country someplace, and we'd have to find somewhere to do it without registering, so it'd be illegal. Probably dangerous too, when they come to slam that old hydrogun against the spine . . . but, hey, I'm friendly, so what the hell?"

"So you'll do it?"

"I guess so."

"You won't be sorry."

She twisted around to put the pod on the bed beside her, then leaned forward to stand up. As she did so he saw that the towel had been working loose again, because for an instant he glimpsed the soft pointed mound of her breast. Once again she clutched the towel against her. She headed for the bathroom.

"Where are you going?" Pikul asked.

"To get dressed. I can't go out half naked."

"So where are we going after that?"

"To get you a bioport."

"What, now? Right away?"

"No time like the present," Geller said.

"What do we do? Just drive up to your local country gas station in the middle of the night?"

"Something like that," she said, and closed the bathroom door. This time she locked it behind her.

[7]

There was a gas station two miles up the highway, and it was open. At least, there was a sign that said it was open. There were three gas pumps outside with lights on, but the building itself was dark.

Pikul stopped the Land Rover by the pumps and held his hand down on the horn for a few seconds.

After a long pause a wooden door in the old building opened and a gangly pump attendant ambled slowly over.

"Fill her up," Pikul said. "Unleaded."

"You got it."

In the light from the pumps Pikul read the young man's name, embroidered on his overalls. He appeared to be called Gas. Gas leaned over the filler cap while the tank filled. He was staring away into the darkness, a low whistling noise sifting through his lips. Pikul and Geller hovered nervously.

When the tank was full, the attendant said, "Anything else I can get for you folks?"

"Well," Geller said, "Gas—is that your name . . . Gas?"

"That's what they call me." He had a halting, country accent; he seemed nervous, but there was an intangible sense of menace arising from him. Pikul found that he was tensing himself.

"Would you check our bioport plugs?" Allegra asked.

"Check your what? You mean check your spark plugs?"

"No . . . you heard me right. My friend here has a bioport problem."

The young man straightened and stared steadily at her. It was the first time they had been able to get a clear look at his face. He had regular, well-chiseled features, but there was a vacancy behind his eyes, a reserve. The way he looked at them now seemed to imply a judgment, but the sheer blankness of the expression in his eyes gave them no chance to sense what it might be.

"A bioport," he said slowly. "Now, that's a kind of hole in your spine, isn't it? There's a lot of *ass*holes around here, but that's generally it. I don't know why you'd be talking to me about that kind of thing, lady."

"Sure you do," Geller said. "I think you might already know who I am."

"Don't get me wrong," the attendant said automatically, "but if you were the First Lady and you came in here looking for an unlicensed bioport I wouldn't be able to fit one for you."

"I'm not the First Lady," Geller said. "But I might be the last."

She moved around so the light from the nearest pump fell on her face. She looked at the young attendant with a level, neutral expression, clearly awaiting his reaction.

He stared back, and as he did so Pikul saw his eyes widen with recognition and disbelief.

Gas pulled a greasy wallet from his overalls and flipped out the card holders. He riffled through them: Pikul glimpsed shots of a family, a fishing photo with three men in waders, a couple of highly polished hot rods with young men standing in front of them. Gas stopped at one particular picture: it was a color photograph of Geller clipped from a glossy magazine. The caption read: ALLEGRA GELLER—GENIUS IN A GAME-POD.

Gas flashed this dismissively at Pikul, like it was a police ID tab, then turned to Geller and in an unexpected blur of moment threw himself at her feet. He stared up at her.

"Allegra Geller," he said in a tone of genuine reverence. "You have changed my life."

He reached over and took her hand in his, then

raised it and gently brushed his lips across her knuckles.

Smiling broadly, Geller essayed a little curtsy. They both burst out laughing.

"I'm Ted Pikul," Pikul said, holding out his hand, but the other two were already walking off side by side toward the garage building.

Into the dark.

Pikul followed them inside to a murky confusion of half-repaired cars, drums of oil, muffler pipes stacked against the wall, piles of tires, racks of tools, lift ramps, chain hoists, hydraulic jacks, tire pressure charts . . . all inefficiently lit by a low-wattage bulb hanging high in the wooden ceiling. Geller glanced around inside.

"I guess I'll go breathe some fresh air," she said to Gas. "While you get Pikul fitted out."

"Yeah, you fit me out," Pikul said.

Gas gave another fond wave to Geller, who went back out to the yard. He then threw a couple of wall switches by the chain-lift hoist and more lights came on in the dingy workshop.

"Are you sure you know how to fit bioports?" Pikul asked.

"Wouldn't admit it to anyone else," Gas said cheerfully. "But I sure do."

"And you fit them in this place?"

"You bet. New tires, new clutches, new batteries,

new brake pads, new spark plugs, new bioports—you name it. Wait here, Pikul, and I'll get ready."

He wandered over to the other side of the workshop, where another pair of overalls was hanging on a hook. He stripped off the set he'd been wearing, then stepped into the others. They didn't look much cleaner than the first pair but at least they didn't have so many holes.

"What was your life like before?" Pikul asked.

"Before what?"

"Before it was changed by Allegra Geller."

"Oh yeah. Well, I operated a gas station and car repair workshop."

"But you still operate a gas station and car repair workshop."

Gas's shoulders tensed, and he turned toward Pikul with a menacing stare. Then he grinned, affability returning like a light switching on.

"Sure I do," he said. "At least, that's what it looks like on the exterior. You can't see beyond that because you're trapped by the most pathetic level of literal reality. Deeper down, on the levels you can't appreciate, Allegra Geller's work liberated me."

"Liberated?"

"Did you ever play her game called ArtGod? One word, capital A, capital G?"

"I don't have a bioport," Pikul said. "Remember?"

"'Thou, the player of the game, thou art God.'"

Gas looked wistful at the memory. "Very spiritual. Funny too. God the artist, God the mechanic. They don't write them like that anymore."

He zipped up his fresh pair of overalls.

"Those are sterile, aren't they?" Pikul said.

Gas glanced down briefly at himself, and brushed his oil-grimed hands over his chest.

"Pretty much," he said. "But you needn't worry. The way they set things up, you could fire in a bioport in a slaughterhouse and still not generate an infection."

"Then why do you need to go through the whole damn thing and change into clean overalls?"

Gas was crossing to the rack of car tools, but Pikul's comment made him pause. It was as if the thought had never occurred to him before. Again Pikul sensed a sudden rising of hostility from the young man, quickly suppressed.

"You know, it's a mental thing," Gas said. "Helps me focus on the task. It psychs me up into hydrogun mode. The one thing you can't afford to do is miss with the stud-finder."

"Oh, God," Pikul said.

"God the artist, God the mechanic," Gas replied, and gave Pikul a big, disingenuous smile.

He rattled around on the rack for a while, lifting things away to see if what he was looking for was underneath. Then he moved to a long workbench cluttered with tools and spare parts, finally finding his red metal rolling toolbox. He pulled open one of its large slide-out drawers.

After another short search, he withdrew a small electronic device, covered in grease and smears, which looked a little like a carbon-fiber voltage meter. It had a metal feeler with a long sharp point, which Gas rubbed absentmindedly against the side of his overall pants. When he was done, he inspected the point against the light, licked his thumb and finger, and smeared the sharpest points. Then he rubbed them again.

He pulled on a pair of industrial shatterproof spectacles.

"We call this baby a stud-finder," Gas said, peering at it through the thick lenses. "It uses a combination of sonar and laser to locate the spot on your spine where the x intersects with the y. We don't want to be even a micron out of whack." He took off the safety spectacles for a moment and blew away some specks of dirt that had built up on the lenses. "One micron off and you get troubles. Spinal damage, paralysis, spasms, uncontrollable pain, that sort of thing."

Pikul briefly closed his eyes.

"But this little baby never goes wrong if you handle it right. It marks you with a special range-finding dye."

"Never say dye," Pikul said, but Gas didn't appear to understand.

"Lift up your shirt," he said humorlessly. "And turn around."

Pikul reluctantly did as he was instructed. He moved forward onto a wingback chair next to one of the workbenches, and at Gas's instruction, settled himself in an awkward kneeling position. He gritted his teeth and waited for the end of the world to begin.

In front of him was a small, grimy window, with a view out across the forecourt. Geller was there, game-pod still slung over her shoulder. She was wandering around in the night, looking about her in what seemed to be a state of awe. She lightly brushed her fingertips against anything she passed: from the rusty remains of broken automobiles to the high-tech Mobil gas pumps.

A stab of white fire entered his spine, and Pikul went rigid with pain.

"See, that didn't hurt, did it?" Gas said.

Pikul tried to answer, but his voice came out as a gassy, high-pitched squeak. He coughed, cleared his throat, blinked away the tears.

"Just a little," he said manfully.

"I told you."

"All right . . . well, thanks for doing that." Pikul moved down from his awkward kneeling position on the chair. He stretched and twisted. Everything began to feel all right again. "How much do I owe you?"

"I haven't done it yet," Gas said. "That was just the

stud-finder. It puts a marking stain on your skin, in the exact place where the bioport has to go."

Pikul bent backward, trying to see over his shoulder. He tried to feel with his hand.

"Don't rub it!" Gas warned him. "One micron off . . . remember?"

He pulled the bioport insertion gun from another drawer. This was much larger than the stud-finder: it had two unpleasant-looking hydraulic levers clamped beside a deadly barrel, with a pump-up mechanism that made a deep-seated ratchet sound when Gas limbered it up.

He snapped something made of metal out of a vacuum-sealed pack and clicked it onto the end of the barrel.

"Back on the chair please, Pikul."

He reluctantly complied. "This is the bit that hurts, right?" he said.

"I've never crippled anyone yet."

"How many have you done?"

"Three," Gas said. "Well, you'll be the third."

Geller walked as far as the Land Rover, then turned back to pass by the other pumps. The stars shone brightly overhead, and a warm wind blew from the west. She breathed the air deeply. For the first time since leaving the church, she was beginning to feel comparatively safe. Yes, the crazies were undoubtedly still out there somewhere looking for her, but it would take them a long time to narrow their search down to this particular filling station on this particular road.

As she glanced around, her attention was suddenly drawn by a movement on the gas pump at the far end. She went over to investigate.

An animal of some kind had crawled up on to the chrome-plated handle of the pump. It sat in the moonlight, twitching in the warm night. She bent down to look more closely.

It was a salamanderlike amphibian with six legs. Its feet were fat and splayed, giving a good grip on the shiny metal. It was constantly moving, twitching from side to side.

It had two heads.

Each head sat on its own neck, and each seemed to be striving for domination over the other. Both the tiny heads were swaying from side to side, banging into each other.

Geller reached down and gently took the tiny thing in her hand. Its little feet briefly clung more tightly to the glistening metal, but then came away with almost inaudible popping sounds. It rested on her palm, its legs spread wide. The heads continued to wave frantically about, causing the animal to stumble whenever it tried to move. It finally discovered the root of her thumb with its tail, and used this to stabilize itself.

She leaned down for a closer look. The little creature's heads suddenly stopped waggling about and both looked back up at Geller through bulging, frog-like eyes.

Then she heard a cry from within the workshop: "Geller, help! *Geller!*"

[8]

Pikul had backed away to the far end of the filthy workshop and was holding a large wrench he'd seized from a rack. Gas stood before him, the bioport insertion gun raised for action. Both men were breathing menacingly at each other.

Geller rushed in from outside. "What's going on, Gas?" she yelled.

He glanced at her over his shoulder. "Your friend is acting like I'm attacking him. People usually pay me to do this, you know."

"Yeah, all two of them!" Pikul cried. "This character's a fucking amateur, Geller. I'm not going ahead with the bioport just so's he can get in some practice on me. That's flat, and it's final."

"What's this about two of them?" Geller said to Gas.

"My little joke," he replied. "Just winding him up a little. Bedside manner, you know."

"Pikul doesn't have much of a sense of humor," Geller said quietly, then pushed past him. She went straight up to Pikul. "No bioport, then?"

"No."

She glanced back at Gas, judging the distance, then lowered her voice to a husky whisper. Her breath played lightly on Pikul's cheek.

"This is it, Pikul, you see," she said. "This is the cage I was talking about, the cage you make for yourself. It keeps you trapped inside, pacing about in the smallest possible space. Forever. You'll never escape because you've forgotten, or you never knew, how you got inside in the first place. This is your chance, Pikul. Break out of your cage. Break out of it now."

He stared back at her, breathing heavily.

"I don't want to," he said stubbornly.

She moved closer still.

"Think of the rewards, Pikul. Think of where we could go together." She was leaning toward him. She plucked at the front of her T-shirt, pulling it forward, making a gap down which he could steal a glimpse. He stole a glimpse. She let go again.

"Everything can be yours," she said. "That's not a promise. It's a prediction."

Kneeling once more on the wingback chair, trembling and shuddering, Pikul waited for the impact. He heard Gas moving around behind him, he sensed something being adjusted, he heard again that deep ratchet sound. Something cold and metal touched his back.

Slam!

Pikul fell forward into the chair, while the agony screamed through his body. Nothing in his life had even approached the threshold of such pain, far less actually crossed it.

Then, remarkably fast, it began to fade.

Within a minute of the terrible impact the area of his lower back felt as if an extremely large and sensitive carbuncle had suddenly grown there, but the shattering, paralyzing pain had receded.

Pikul wondered if he should continue to lie in the humiliating facedown position in the chair awhile longer, to ram home his point about having to suffer, then decided against it. Slowly, he eased himself around. His eyes focused.

Gas and Geller were watching him. He fancied that Geller was watching him with concern and affection, but he couldn't be too sure of that.

"Okay, Pikul," Gas said. "You're going to have a swelling there for a few hours, but by tomorrow you won't even notice it."

"I love it," Pikul said. "Great."

He tried to get up from the wingback chair but the moment he put weight on his legs he collapsed forward into the arms of Geller and Gas.

"What's going on?" he cried in panic. "I can't walk!"

Geller helped Gas ease him back into a sitting position in the chair.

"The bioport comes with its own epidural, like when you have a baby," Gas said.

"I don't have babies."

"If you did, you'd be familiar with the feeling. Instant paralysis from the waist down."

"Paralysis?" Pikul said, thinking of several important parts of his body from the waist down.

"Only temporary. You wouldn't want to experience the full pain of invasive spinal tapping, would you? The epidural saves you from pain. It'll wear off in no time."

Pikul noticed that there were specks of fresh blood and tiny flecks of skin on Gas's work gloves. A mist of tiny blood droplets lay on the lenses of his safety glasses.

"You look more like a butcher than a mechanic," he said.

"Things do get kind of confused these days, don't they?" Gas said, but he made no attempt to wipe off the stains. A smile formed on his mouth, beneath his cold, empty eyes. "I'm going to go wash up. You two make yourselves at home."

He threw his gloves to one side and strode off in the direction of the washroom. He was emanating great waves of self-satisfaction.

Geller shifted the game-pod case from her shoulder and eased the pod out. She started attaching a Y-shaped two-player UmbyCord to it.

"What are you doing?" Pikul said.

"We don't have to wait for the swelling to go down."

"You're going to port into me? While I'm still paralyzed?"

"Sure I am."

"In this dump?" Pikul waved his hand helplessly in all directions, at the greasy chaos of the place.

"It doesn't matter where we are in the real world. It's the game that counts."

"Yes, but—"

Geller paused in what she was doing and moved so she could look directly at him.

"You still want to play my game, don't you?" she said.

"Yeah . . . I did and I do. But come on, Allegra. Play games here in this repair shop? Now? With God the Mechanic in the next room?"

"No time like the present, is there?"

She reached forward and lifted his unbuttoned shirt, peering behind him at the base of his spine.

"It's beautiful," she said.

To Pikul's amazement, she leaned over and began to caress the port with her face, rubbing her cheeks, lips, and hair over it, making satisfied grunting sounds deep inside her throat. Finally, with a quiet sucking noise, she took the port in her mouth.

Pikul felt almost none of this, because of the anesthetic effect of the epidural, but he heard it all and imagined the rest. If his below-the-belt responses hadn't been temporarily wiped out of existence, he would have had an unequivocal below-the-belt response to this. He glanced down at Geller's back, could just see her head bobbing sexily as she mouthed the port with her tongue and lips.

More embarrassed than aroused, Pikul waited until she was content. Then she leaned away from him, took out a tiny aerosol can of WD–40 from her game-pod case, and sprayed it on him.

"Ouch! That's cold!"

"A new port is sometimes a bit tight. It's difficult to get the connector in. I wouldn't want to hurt you."

"How come a bioport . . . ?" Pikul began, having given this a little thought. "How come a bioport doesn't get infected? I mean, it opens right into your body. Shouldn't you be using antiseptic instead of that stuff?"

"Don't be ludicrous."

"Ludicrous?"

"Listen to what you're saying, Pikul."

"I listen to me," he said. "Sometimes I think I'm the only one who does. Look, Geller, I don't mind admitting I'm kind of nervous about this. I'm here in this hellhole, great gobbets of filth and machine oil around me, a maniac with blood on his hands has just carried out spine surgery on me, now you want us to roll around on the floor together."

"Get out of your cage, Pikul . . . "

"Don't you think you could at least call me Ted?" he said. "You know, help me through all this?"

"Maybe later," she said, absorbed in what she was doing.

Geller was gently working the connector of the UmbyCord into Pikul's new bioport. He felt her tapping it reassuringly when it was properly seated, then she moved around to face him and looked intently into his eyes.

She reached down and squeezed her game-pod's On teat.

Instantly, the pod convulsed! White flashes sparked and crackled around its body. Electronic smoke seeped from its crevices and a kind of bioelectronic fat sputtered from the many pores that pitted its surface.

"My God!" Geller cried in horror.

She leaped away from him and yanked her UmbyCord out of his bioport with such a force that it jerked him around in his chair. He felt no pain, just the sheer physical pulling of her frantic action.

"Shit, Pikul!" she said furiously. "I can't believe this. I trusted you, and in return you blew my pod! You must have neurosurged."

"I must have—what? What do you mean? Neuro-surged . . . what's that?"

"I jacked you into my pod," she said, in a tone of despair. "You panicked and you neurosurged. Now the pod is totally fucked! You've no idea what a disaster this is going to be for me!"

"I was nervous . . . that's right. I was real nervous. But I didn't panic."

"You blew my pod!"

"Your pod blew. Okay, I'm not arguing. But why blame me for it?"

"You were there," Geller said, with cold reason. "It was jacked into you, and then it blew."

"Couldn't you get a new one?"

She looked at him with disbelief, and for a moment he thought she was going to burst out in some way: tears, hysterical laughter, great rage. Then she lowered her eyes and sadness briefly dwelled in her face.

She crouched before him, cradling the pod.

"Pikul, in this pod is the only, the original, version of *eXistenZ*. It's an entire game system, and it cost thirty-eight million dollars to develop, not including prerelease marketing costs. Now I'm locked outside my own game! I can't get it out, or me in!"

"Are you serious?" he said. "This is the only version of the software there is?"

"*eXistenZ* isn't software. You can back up software.

eXistenZ is a whole, living system! You can't make copies of living systems. Security is everything these days. It's the only version, and it's stuck inside and it's your fault." Geller used her sleeve to clean the drool off the pod. She moved with tragic gentleness, as if treating an injured child. "I've given my five most passionate years to this strange little creature," she went on. "I've never regretted it, Pikul, because I knew it was the only thing that could give my life any meaning."

"But why is it my fault? I'm telling you I didn't, I did not, definitely did not neurosurge. I didn't feel any neurosurging."

Gas now strolled back into the workshop. He was holding, almost casually, a long shotgun. It was leveled at Geller.

"You can relax, Pikul," he said. "It wasn't your fault. It was mine."

Pikul's instincts to act in protection of Geller swarmed over him, but he was still physically paralyzed. He writhed in a futile way in the chair. Geller backed away from Gas, clutching her game-pod protectively.

"Oh no, Gas!" she cried. "Not you!"

"Yeah, I guess it was." For a moment he looked uncertain of what he intended. With his free hand he swept back the hair that had fallen loosely down across his sweating face. "I wouldn't try using that bioport again. Except maybe as a toaster or something."

"What's going on, Gas?" Geller asked.

"You're worth a lot of money if you're dead."

"What are you talking about?" Pikul said.

"You know what I'm talking about. It's all over the country, on every TV show and news bulletin. Five million for your dead body. No questions asked."

"But she changed your life!" Pikul said, trapped in his chair.

"Yup . . . and now I think I'm gonna change hers."

"But wait, Gas! Why did you install that faulty bioport into me?"

"It seems that as well as the five mil, there's an extra bonus for killing Allegra Geller's latest game system. I think I just did that too, didn't I?"

Geller had stopped backing away. Pikul saw a new, hard expression in her face. She walked slowly, carefully, toward Gas, desperate not to provoke a sudden reaction.

"But can you actually kill a person in cold blood, Gas?" Geller asked. "Can you really do that? Can you kill me?"

"Sure I can," he said.

"Okay, let's say you do it." For a moment her voice faltered, but then she went on. "You hide my body someplace out back. You contact the crazies who put up the ransom. You trust them to pay up. You give them my now-decaying, fucking grotesque corpse. Do you really expect them to hand over the five mil cash? Without the feds getting interested? Without some kind of cheesy double cross? Don't you ever go to the fucking movies?"

"I like your script, Geller," Gas said. "I've always liked the story lines in your games. Yeah, they're life-changing, like I said. I want that one you just ran by me, I want to be in on it."

He cocked the shotgun, tightened his finger on the trigger.

At the same time, there was the sound of a deep-seated ratchet. Gas's face twitched in recognition. He paused, started to turn around.

Too long! Pikul fired the bioport insertion gun, shooting Gas in the mastoid bone behind his right ear. The back of Gas's skull shattered messily and car repair tools dislodged by the spasmic swinging of his arm crashed to the floor. The shotgun flew away from him and wheeled and clattered across the dirty work-shop.

Pikul threw down the gun and thrust himself out of the chair. Once again his legs could not take his weight and he fell to the ground beside Gas's body. Blood was pouring out of the man's head wound, spreading darkly across the greasy concrete floor.

"Oh God, I think he's dead!" Pikul said unnecessarily. "I only meant to distract him."

"He's distracted all right," Geller said. She looked down contemptuously at the body of the dead mechanic. "Plug your goddamn toaster into *that* hole, corpse!"

[9]

They drove through the night. More accurately, Geller drove and Pikul hung on. He was starting to feel the return of sensation in his below-the-belt region, the most agonizing and widespread attack of pins and needles he'd ever known.

Propped up in the passenger seat of the Land Rover, he said, "Gas was going to kill you."

"You noticed!" She afforded him a sardonic glance.

"That's two people in one day who seriously wanted to kill you."

"I've never been more popular."

"Don't mess with this," Pikul said. "People who want to kill you don't seem to care if I'm caught in the cross fire."

"You're a trained bodyguard. The new generation, you told me."

"I guess I meant I was a trainee. I'm not used to so much violence. I live a quiet life."

"So do I," said Geller. "You want to know how I normally live when I'm not been chased about the country by a bunch of crazies?"

"Tell me."

She said nothing for what seemed like several minutes. Pikul said nothing more to prompt her, already knowing her well enough to realize that at least half the time he was misreading her intentions. When he looked across at her, she was staring ahead at the road as she drove, biting thoughtfully on her bottom lip.

"Okay, I live in a community out on Highway 11," she said eventually. "Where the lake country begins. You know it? Well, it's real pretty and it's real lonely. The community has about fifteen people. They come and go, but that's about the average. We do a few things as a group: buy groceries, for instance. But that's about it. I have a studio at the back end of the area: I'm completely surrounded by trees, and I'm cut off from the other buildings by a small river. Out back of my studio is the lake. I can go a week, two weeks, and never see anyone, if I don't want."

"No TV?"

"I don't watch TV. Just videos. But I don't even watch them too often. What I mostly do is work. I love work. I eat and sleep and drink work. It's my life. I have in my studio the most advanced games simulator in the country, and out back, in a special building, I have all the organ development matrices I need, where the pod can be nurtured. That's my life, Pikul: I just descend every day into the virtual world and write my game and pander to the needs of the pod."

"Doesn't sound real to me."

"Well, I get a paycheck once a month. Does that help you understand a bit better?"

"Only from Antenna Research," Pikul intoned.

"Right. But the point is, I don't live in a world where people issue death threats and come at you with a gun made out of a dead animal. I live with nature, and the people around me are artists, craftsmen, designers, thinkers. We feel we are part of a global movement away from crime and violence, developing into a higher state of being."

"Sounds great," Pikul said sardonically. "So long as you're not poor, not living in a deprived area of a big city, not ill, not mentally unfit, not—"

"Okay, okay, I take your point. I'm not saying we're living a life everyone should lead. I know I'm privileged. But my work brings a lot of pleasure to millions of people, and what I do is essentially harmless. We can't all live in a cabin by a lake. But some of us do, and I'm one of them . . . and it's no preparation for exposure to a wider world, where people scream your name and come at you with hate in their eye."

"I keep thinking about that," Pikul said.

"I know. So do I."

Pikul, in a melancholy mood, considered the situation as the countryside raced past the car windows. Was this to be the rest of his life, fleeing across the highways and back roads of rural areas?

"Allegra, we need help," he said eventually.

"Now you're talking. I've got to get this pod fixed."

The pins and needles had set in with total commitment as Pikul stared dimly through the windshield at the lightening sky. Geller still drove at high speed as the sun came up, when Pikul, exhausted by the events of the long night, at last began to snooze.

He drifted in a state of half sleep for a long time, the engine droning on, its steady rhythm broken intermittently by an occasional lurch for a corner or a junction or a hole in the road. But he could relax like this, in this big comfortable machine designed for the wide roads and the rough country.

When the Land Rover started lurching violently, its engine working hard, he opened his eyes and saw they were climbing a narrow dirt track. Great mountains rose around them. Tall firs blotted out the closer views, but the smell of pine and resin and flowers hit Pikul like a restorative shot. The air was colder, fresher, and the sky bluer. He sat up in the seat, suddenly alert. Whether there was feeling in his legs was a debatable point, but he realized he could make some movements again.

They reached a pair of stone gateposts, which bore a coy, rustic sign: CALEDON SKI CLUB—PRIVATE ROAD.

"Are you taking me skiing?" he asked her in disbelief.

"Hi. Welcome back to planet Earth. You've been out for a couple of hours."

He struggled around in his seat, looking at the skyline, the bare slopes high above them.

"I'm maybe fit for living," he ventured, "but not for skiing."

"Relax," Geller said. "Nothing in the countryside is what it seems. It's all appearance versus reality. The reality here is something unique."

After another mile of climbing they reached a large A-frame chalet, standing back from the track and surrounded by tall firs. Geller turned off the engine and climbed down.

With more of a struggle, Pikul managed to get his legs dangling vertically from the seat toward the ground. When he lowered his weight onto them, he discovered he was able to stand, after a fashion. He held on to the large side mirror sticking out from the door.

A movement caught his eye, and he noticed something black and slithery fingering its way across the convex glass of the mirror.

"Hey, look at this huge bug!" he called to Geller,

who was already walking up toward the chalet. She turned back and came to see. "The goddamn thing's got two heads."

"It's not a bug," she said, bending down to look closely at it. "I saw one of those last night. Might even be the same one, coming along for the ride. It's a mutated amphibian, a frog-salamander-lizard thing."

"I can tell you've checked it out in a reference book. It still looks like a bug to me."

"It's a sign of the times," Geller said, shrugging.

Pikul closed the door gingerly, not wanting to shake the little amphibian off its perch, then followed Geller as she walked up the path toward the chalet. His legs felt weird, but he kept upright and managed not to fall.

She slowed, to let him catch up with her.

Glancing around at the magnificent mountain scenery, he said, "What if somebody comes up here and really wants to ski?"

"They can ski."

"I thought you said it was appearance and not reality."

"Right. Nobody actually skis anymore. You know, sliding down a snow-covered mountain on polished slats of wood? You realize that, don't you?"

"Uh-huh."

"You haven't realized that," she said.

"I've watched some ski shows on TV. Downhill

racing, Austrian Alps, Garmisch-Partenkirchen, and all that."

"Yeah, right."

"What the hell's wrong with that?" Pikul asked, aggravated by the tone of contempt in her voice.

"There's reality, there's what you see on TV, and there's virtual reality. Guess which one is going to win the day?"

She pushed open the unlocked door and they both entered the chalet.

To Pikul's eye, most of the interior did at least look the way he expected a ski-repair workshop might: there were skis everywhere in various states of repair and repainting, as well as vices, lathes, saw benches, and dozens of long wooden racks holding new pairs of skis.

In the center, though, were three worktables, not at all the kind of thing you expected would be used to make or repair skis. The large slabs with porcelain work surfaces seemed more suited to a mortuary. Gleaming surgical instruments were laid out neatly, held in special racks. Huge overhead angle-lights with diffusers added to the impression of an operating theater.

Their arrival must have been overheard, Pikul thought, as the door to a back room opened. The man who appeared looked to be in his early sixties. He seemed distinguished, authoritarian in manner, and his bright blue eyes were crinkly and alert.

He recognized Geller immediately and his face creased with pleasure at seeing her.

"My darling Allegra!" He spoke in a pronounced East European accent. He held out his arms in welcome, and she went to him. They kissed cheeks, then embraced warmly. "I am so pleased to see you! And astonished!"

"Kiri, I want you to meet my bodyguard, Ted Pikul. Ted, this is Kiri Vinokur, one of my oldest and closest friends."

"It's good to meet you, Ted."

"You too, sir. I guess you should just call me Pikul."

"A bodyguard, you are saying?" Kiri Vinokur frowned. "This sounds serious. Maybe more serious than I had been thinking. I hear the ridiculous story about a *fatwa* issuing against you. The company is trying desperately to be finding you. Is it really as serious as this? Are you in danger?"

Pikul said, "She seems to think that since I've become her bodyguard she's in more danger."

"There have been a couple of attempts on my life already."

"No! That's unbearable. The company must be stopping this. They are owing you every kind of protection."

"I don't know what they can do about it. These people are crazy. It seems to be open season on me."

"My dear, safe here you will be." Vinokur waved his hands expansively, taking in the interior of the chalet and the surrounding mountainous valley. "I can assure you of that. I shall be contacting Antenna straight away and be having them send some people to come and collect you."

Geller looked agitated.

"No, Kiri," she said. "Don't do that, however good your intentions. You mustn't let anybody know we're here. I can't be sure anymore that Antenna is completely safe for me."

Vinokur shook his head with great sadness.

"It has come to this, then. Finally. I understand, I suppose. The company has always been having the bad habit of drawing brilliant and eccentric people into its fold. You and your, er, bodyguard can of course be hiding out here for as long as you like. Several of the guest chalets are free at present. I will make sure you are having fresh towels."

"Thanks, Kiri!" Geller said. She patted her game-pod case. "But, you know, I've really come so you can make sure I don't lose everything I have in here."

[10]

Later, when they'd settled in, Kiri Vinokur got to work on Geller's game-pod. He laid it out systematically on the porcelain work surface, using in the first instance a number of dexterous manual handling techniques Pikul could not quite follow. The man's hands moved swiftly and expertly, like those of a professional masseur. He finally opened the organism up, so it lay spread before him.

Next, the operation itself began. In this, Vinokur was assisted by a technician called Landry, a cherubic-faced middle-aged man. Using his special electronic diagnostic tools, which had the approximate appearance of scalpels that apparently did not make actual physical contact with the pod, Vinokur began the painstaking work of determining what might have happened to the cybernetic brain inside.

"What on earth did you port into, Allegra?" he

said, glancing up at Geller over his special clip-on magnifying spectacle lenses.

"Pikul's bioport," she replied.

"Really? And could it be that's what is causing all this damage, you are thinking?"

"The installation was flawed," Pikul hastily explained. "It was my first time. The port . . . well, it neurosurged. That's a phenomenon you're familiar with, of course. We're pretty sure of it, anyway. But it did it all on its own, without me. Allegra says you can fix it."

"Whatever happened," Vinokur said, "it fried some expensive neural webbing. You are seeing?" He was indicating a red/pink pulsing node of cybersynapses. He circled the area with the tip of his electronic scalpel. "Here . . . and here. This cord of response tissue. All this is *kaput*."

Pikul said, "It looks like an animal lying down there. To me it feels like you're operating on somebody's pet dog."

Geller and Vinokur exchanged a strange look. Then, abruptly, Vinokur laughed.

"See?" he said to Landry. "I told you it is glorified veterinarians we have become." He gave Pikul a more respectful nod. "The *eXistenZ* game-pod is indeed basically animal in origin, Mr. Pikul. It was cloned from fertilized amphibian eggs, gene-spliced from species-related living organic material. Plus, how shall I say?, a certain *stuffing* of our own. Synthetic DNA resins they are, mostly. What is making a pod different from the animals is its brain, and of course its memory. The remembering is the key. An awful lot of sophisticated nanotechnology is building into this baby."

Another look passed between the three of them.

"Only from Antenna Research," Geller said after a moment, and they all laughed.

"Okay," Pikul said, feeling he was being let in on a joke for once. "Where do the batteries go?"

"Very amusing."

Geller said, "He's not kidding. In spite of appearances, he's not just a bodyguard nerd. He's a total PR nerd too."

"Hey, I'm just trying to keep up," Pikul protested. "You've been working with *eXistenZ* for years."

"Okay, I'm sorry." Geller touched the part of his back where the bioport was and let her fingers linger there a few moments, her touch almost affectionate. "We get so close to our work, we always forget how strange it can seem to people who are fresh to it. The MetaFlesh pod ports into you, and *you* become the power source. Your body, your nervous system, your metabolism, your immune system. Basically, it's your energy. When you get tired, run-down, the pod won't function properly."

While she was speaking, Vinokur was looking all over the body of the pod, his hands raised out of the way. A last visual inspection, just to make sure.

"All right," he said after he'd completed the check. "Mr. Landry here will finish up the pod work."

"It's going to be okay?" Geller asked, simply.

"My dear," Vinokur said, and suddenly laughed aloud, an abrupt and mirthless burst of sound. He was looking away from her. He paused, staring for a moment out of the window at the distant views of the snowcapped mountains. "You know how we are here in this place! Better than new. Always better than you begin. Trust me. Yes, I am realizing already you must trust me . . . otherwise you wouldn't be here."

"Right."

"Right," Kiri Vinokur said, nodding happily. "I'm glad we are still on the same wavelength we always were. Now then . . ." He turned to Pikul. "Mr. Pikul."

"Yes?"

"We are not wanting any more neurosurges, are we?"

"Sir, I tell you again, it wasn't me who—"

"Yes, yes, I am hearing what you said." The man looked testy, somewhat dangerous. He breathed in, and flexed the knuckles of both hands. Curiously, no clicking sound could be heard. "We have agreed it is not you who caused the damage. I am more concerning with what it is that is damaging you."

"Me?" Pikul said, with a worried glance in Geller's direction. She signaled with a small hand movement not to respond. "Okay. Tell me what you must," he said to Vinokur.

"I think it's time to get that nasty diseased bioport out of you and replace it with one that isn't going to do any more harm."

"But I'm kind of getting used to it now, sir," Pikul said, alarmed at this unexpected turn of events.

"No, it's doing you no good there. No good at all. All that adverse biofeedback going into your bloodstream. Even a few more hours could be inducing antibody reactions that will take weeks to throw off. I'm not trying to scare you, but we're talking about the possibility of death here."

"You're scaring me," Pikul said.

"Well, it's not likely to come to that," Vinokur said. "We are here to be helping. But we don't want any more adverse publicity, do we? Any of us. Now, where did I put my bioport puller . . . ? Here it is."

He produced from one of the lathe benches an instrument that to Pikul's horrified eyes looked like a pair of spring-loaded fire tongs.

"Mr. Pikul, if you would be good enough to lie down on that couch. And kindly pull up your shirt."

Pikul saw the look in Geller's eyes, and with a feeling of terminal dread reluctantly complied.

[11]

Standing in front of the full-length mirror in the guest chalet, Pikul twisted and strained to see the effect the new bioport had had on his sore, tormented back.

To his largely uninitiated eyes, the new bioport implanted by Kiri Vinokur appeared much the same as the one it had replaced, but the area of skin and flesh around the incision looked and felt swollen, bruised, and tender.

He touched it gingerly with a fingertip.

"It hurts like hell," he said to Geller, who was looking intently at her repaired game-pod nestling in its case. "I think it's infected."

"Does it hurt the same way as the one Gas put in?"

"No . . . it's found another way of hurting. It's different."

"Then apart from the fact that Gas probably caused a little short-term collateral damage to the skin around the port, it sounds normal." She went over and peered at it, but after a superficial glance merely shook her head. She straightened so she could face him, and looked serious and thoughtful. "I don't think the port is infected. It's just excited. I believe it wants a bit of action."

She rubbed her fingers over it lightly, as you would the head of a child you wanted to encourage. To Pikul's surprise, this did not hurt at all.

Geller went back to her game-pod and brought out the Y-shaped UmbyCord. She tried to jack one end of it into his new bioport.

Pikul twisted adroitly away from her. "Hey, how about me?" he said. "I really don't think that *I'm* ready for action. Me, I mean. You know, the bearer of the excited bioport. What I want is . . . not now. Not here. I feel too . . . exposed. Anyway, can't we have a break from all this? I'm hungry, we've traveled a long way—"

"You're not panicking again, are you?" Geller said. "Not likely to neurosurge again?"

"It wasn't me the first time! I keep telling you."

"Yeah, well. The position is that my baby here has now taken three major hits, one back at the church hall, one at the gas station, and one on the operating table. I've got to find out if everything's okay. If the game hasn't been contaminated, the pod hasn't been fucked, that kind of thing. The only way I can do that is to play *eXistenZ* with somebody friendly. Are you still friendly or are you not?"

"I thought we'd already agreed that I was," Pikul said.

He swallowed nervously, then, with a feeling of resignation, turned his back to Geller so she could port in. Unable to see her without twisting his head, he sensed her moving around behind him: her fingers brushed his flesh again, a few strands of her hair fell against his shoulder as she leaned over him. At last he felt the connector jack into his port with a quiet but emphatic mechanical clicking. No trouble there, no pain, no humiliating collapse of his legs.

"How does that feel?" Geller said.

"Okay so far. Are you saying this thing will run off my body's energy?"

"That's how they work." She connected the other end to the game-pod. "See? You're humming along already."

Something was certainly happening. Pikul watched with interest as Geller expertly twisted the second jack into her own bioport, and took a deep breath.

"All right," she said. "*eXistenZ*. Only from Antenna Research. Here we go."

"This is a game, right?" Pikul said.

"Yes."

"We play to win?"

"That's the general idea."

"Then don't you think you've got a bit of an

unfair advantage over me? How can I possibly compete against the person who designed the game?"

"You could beat the guy who invented poker, couldn't you?"

"Not if he didn't tell me all the rules."

"There are no rules in *eXistenZ* that you need to know."

"Then I guess—"

But Geller had flicked the nipple on the gamepod, and before Pikul could finish his answer, the chalet began to melt away around them. The walls thinned out, light shone, light faded. Reality shifted.

[12]

They were standing. They were together. They were inside a building. They were inside a room inside a building. There were people around and many racks of things, but for a few seconds it was impossible to make sense of what they were seeing or even to work out where they might be.

Pikul looked anxiously at Geller, and she looked back.

"So far so good?" he said to her.

"Yes."

"Where are we?"

"I don't know yet."

"We seem to be inside someplace."

"That's okay. We'll survive."

As the sensation of the reality shift faded, Pikul said, "That was a beautiful experience. I feel . . . just like I always feel! Is that normal? I mean is that how games always start? A kind of smooth dissolve from place to place?"

"That's how it goes. It depends on the style of the game. You can get jagged, brutal cuts that shock you into responsive action. You get that kind of thing in the martial arts games, or the explore-and-conquer games. Others are slow fades. I find those pretty frightening, because you don't know what's going to come when it goes all black. It could be the peacefulness of a sea lying under the moon, or a quiet stretch of country-side . . . or it could be a dark cellar where something's lurking and about to leap out on you. Those slow fades always freak me out, just a little. Then you can make shimmering little morphs. Or sideways inserts. There are a lot of options. Everyone does something differ-ent, puts their own style-stamp on their work. Me, I prefer the dissolve."

Pikul was staring away from her, around the large room in which they had found themselves.

"I'm starting to get orientated," he said.

"Me too," Geller said, looking about her with interest.

They were in a retail store, a cramped, scruffy one. Not an especially small store, but an overcrowded one. Narrow aisles led between dusty racks crammed with software and games package boxes labeled in bright colors. There were pinball machines in every available spare spot, and the kids leaning over these were setting up a cacophony of mechanical clattering, signal bells and electronic bleeps. Lights were flashing everywhere.

The customers, prowling along the aisles, kept handling the products, taking them down, looking closely at the small print, turning over the boxes to read what might be printed on the reverse. Most of them were muttering secretively, sometimes to one of the others, most often to themselves.

Pikul and Geller squeezed their way along the aisle in which they were, trying to remove themselves from the press of unwashed bodies.

At the far end a cashier was working behind an old-fashioned cash register that was sitting on a tall counter. He eyed them suspiciously from time to time, but in general was kept busy looking intently at the mass of customers, presumably watching for attempts at theft.

When they passed in front of the counter, Pikul noticed that the young man—gangly and sallow in appearance, like many of the customers—was wearing a name tag. He was identified as Hugo Carlaw.

They went into another aisle, not as crowded as the first.

"Have you worked out where we are yet?" Pikul asked.

"Yeah, now that I can see it more clearly, it's easy. I'm stunned! It's so realistic! This is the game store I used to go to when I was a kid. The very one! This is exactly how I remember it! I'm amazed! It belongs to a Mr. Nadger or Nadder, or some strange, foreign-sounding name like that. I would hang out here for hours when I was a teenager, hoping for a chance to jack into one of the games." She nodded toward a row of consoles where many young people crowded around the brightly lit and constantly changing color screens. "Just like most of these people, in fact," she said.

"Are you serious? This is where you were years ago?"

"No, it's not real. It's a simulation. Remember, we're ported together in the game-pod. *eXistenZ* has complete access to both our central nervous systems. The games architecture we experience in the game will be based on our memories, our anxieties, our preoccupations . . . "

"Not ours," Pikul said. "Yours maybe."

"At the moment my memories are probably predominating. But that isn't necessarily the rule, and your unconscious can and will take over at any time. It's just that I'm more used to the game than you, I know some of the moves. You'll catch on soon enough."

"Are you serious?"

"You keep saying that. Let's have a look at some of this stuff." She turned to the nearest rack and

"I'm warning you, it's going to be a wild ride."

"You're worth a lot of money. If you're dead."

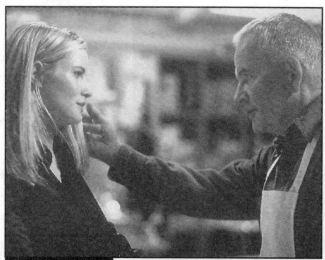

"My darling Allegra. I am so pleased to see you here."

"See? I told you we had become just glorified veterinarians."

"Are you friendly, or are you not?"

"I, ah . . . I've been trained by the very best."

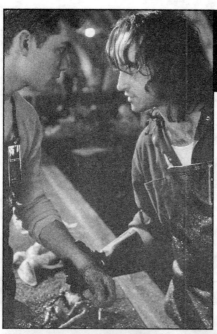

"I do suggest that you order the special. And don't take no for an answer."

"But you *know*, don't you? It's your game, your little universe."

"I feel the urge to kill someone here."

"I found this in my soup and I'm very upset."

"There's a very weird reality bleed-through happening here."

"Oh, yes. We know who you are. You can't hide inside a game forever."

"Death to the demon Yevgeny Nourish! Death to PilgrImage! Death to *TranscendenZ!*"

Jude Law is Ted Pikul, security guard turned fugitive.

Jennifer Jason Leigh is Allegra Geller, world's greatest game designer and creator of *eXistenZ*.

Writer/director David Cronenberg

began sifting through the packages on display. "Look at this. Games I've never even heard of. *Biological Father*. What the hell kind of game could that be? *Hit By a Car* . . . not much imagination needed for that one! *Shop Rage. Theme Supermarket. Landlords on the Rampage. Beastmaster of Avalon. Viral Ecstasy. Chinese Restaurant*."

"The excitement is mounting," Pikul said sardonically. "I can hardly wait to play *Biological Father* . . . a shoot-'em-up arcader, right?"

"Listen to this." Geller was reading the back of the *Viral Ecstasy* box. "When you play this, you get to invade a specific human body—you can choose from a whole library of historical characters—then you create ingenious viral strategies to cope with the efforts of the body's immune system to destroy you . . . "

"That sounds like it's about as much fun as having our friend Gas put in a sicko bioport."

"It's just one of the games I picked up at random," she said defensively.

"Not entirely randomly. Not if it comes from your subconscious."

"It might have come from yours," she pointed out.

"Oh," said Pikul, who hadn't thought of that. He swiftly changed tack. "Look, can you explain something to me? All this stuff on these racks reminds me of what we're doing. We're in a game, okay, but what precisely is the goal of the game?"

"To win," she said. "To finish the game ahead of the game. Nothing special about it."

"No, I mean what's the objective?" Pikul persisted. "What are the rules? You keep going on about how wonderful *eXistenZ* is, but you've never actually said anything about what it *does*."

"Not all games do something."

"You play them to do something."

"No you don't. Some you just play."

"Okay, I'll grant you that. There aren't likely to be a lot of thrills in *Biological Father*. Or none that I can imagine, anyway. But that game isn't state of the art. Your game supposedly is. What's the objective, how do you win?"

She sighed, looking him in the eye as if to try to determine how seriously he meant the questions. She allowed her hand to play lightly across some of the blister packs while she answered.

"The beauty of *eXistenZ*," she said, "is that it changes every time you play it. It adapts to the individuals who are playing it. The result is that you have to play the game to find out why you're playing the game."

"But that's kind of cheating, isn't it?" Pikul said stubbornly. "Not to say confusing."

"It's not confusing at all. And it's not a cheat. *eXistenZ* takes a much more organic approach to gaming than the classic, arbitrary, rule-dominated games. It's the future, Pikul. You'll see how natural it feels. Where we are now . . . doesn't this feel natural?"

"You mean this shop for computer geeks is the *future?*"

Pikul shrugged his shoulders expressively, trying to show the antagonism he felt toward the dozens of intent game customers crowding the aisles of the store. None of them showed any reaction; indeed, hardly any of them showed any awareness that he and Geller were even present.

Pikul looked around and saw something half familiar lying on the shelf beside him. It was a game-pod. He picked it up and showed it to Geller.

"Did you ever see anything like this before?" he asked.

The pod was contained within a gel-pak that was even more bizarre and otherworldly than Geller's own tissue pod. They both examined it with interest. It seemed lumpier than Geller's, less well-integrated or developed. Although the flesh was as venous as her pod's, there did not appear to be the same underlying organic logic, the sense that it had been ripped somehow from a living being. This pod had an arbitrary, thrown-together feeling. They turned it around in their hands, then over on its back. On the underside they came across a corporate logo, and a name: *COR-TICAL SYSTEMATICS.*

A hand reached between them, from behind, and

gently but firmly took the pak away from them. They turned to see who it was.

The man was large and bulky, with thinning gray hair. He had a pugnacious air and seemed irritated that they'd been showing such interest in the game-pod. Swinging from his jacket lapel was a name badge: D'ARCY NADER.

"This game-pods are most delicate," he said, in an accent even more fractured and alien than Kiri Vinokur's. "I'll haff to ask you more careful to be, when you are hantling them."

"We weren't doing any harm," Geller said. "We're just interested customers."

"Ma'am, I do unterstand. But in common wit many retail outlets, we haff to be careful of pilferage and breakings."

"Yes," Pikul said. "I can imagine."

"You know vat a game-pod is?"

"Sure. We've just never seen that one before."

"Cortical Systematics ist the latest and hottest player. Ist not just a new game, but a whole new system."

Pikul said, "Yeah yeah, I've heard all—"

"Will it work with an industry standard bioport?" Geller said, deftly interrupting him.

But Nader was looking more carefully and curiously at them.

"I haffn't see you two around this place before, haff I?" he said.

"Well, no—"

"This ist my place. *Haimische*, isn't it? Funky?"

"Yes, well, we're new in town," Pikul said. "Whichever town this is—"

"Welcome to D'Arcy Nader's Game Emporium," he said. "I am D'Arcy Nader, as you might haff noticed, and I'll be plissed to help you with anything you might be interested in."

"Thank you," Geller said. "But at the moment we're just looking."

Nader glanced along the aisle, side to side.

"I think I might haff what you're looking for," he said softly.

"You do?" Pikul said.

"Follow me, pliss."

Nader turned away from them and stepped along the aisle toward the back of the store. Here, there was a warped and grimy door, with no sign on it.

Nader pushed it partly open, then beckoned urgently to Geller and Pikul. A couple of the other customers saw him signaling and seemed about to go along too. Nader gave them a warning look.

Geller went through the door first, with Pikul following. Before the door closed behind them, Pikul happened to look back. He saw that Hugo Carlaw, the sour-faced cashier they'd noticed when they arrived, was writing something down on a pad of paper. He looked vengeful and self-important.

↔   ↔   ↔

Beyond the door was a dimly lit stockroom, jammed to overflowing with crates and cartons. Long and high vertical racks held a dizzying range of components for computers, old-fashioned game consoles, and parts of organware, nakedly scattered about in varying stages of construction or repair.

Nader indicated some wooden crates, and Geller and Pikul sat down on two of them, feeling disconcerted by Nader's sudden air of menace. He prowled around them for a moment, then took down two more gel-paks from a shelf.

He studied Pikul and Geller, hefting the paks in his hands.

"All right," he said. "Who vos it that sent you?"

"None of your damn business, I'd say," Pikul retorted. "We're here and that's all that matters."

Pikul heard himself say the words, and felt a jolt of surprise. Had he disrupted the game already?

"Hey, Pikul," Geller said softly beside him. "Don't blow it."

"Blow what?"

"The game," she said. "What else?"

"God, what happened? I didn't mean to say that!"

Geller was looking strained, but to his relief, she laughed.

"I guess it wasn't you," she said, "but your character. The game version of you said that. It's a kind of schizophrenic feeling, isn't it? But you'll get used to it soon enough. There are certain things that have to be said by the game players to advance the plot and establish the characters. Those things get said whether you want to say them or not. The trick is not to fight the sensation when it comes. Go with it."

"Okay," Pikul said, feeling somewhat better. "But what you just said . . . should you be saying that in front of him? In front of Nader?"

"Look at him. He's in memory-save mode."

Pikul glanced back. Nader didn't appear to have heard or reacted to anything. He was still standing with the gel-paks in his hands, waiting for a reply to his question. His eyes were closed and he was humming the Antenna Research corporate theme song. His only movements were a slight rhythmic waggling of his head and a foot-tapping motion.

"What's he doing?" Pikul asked.

"He's gone into a game-loop. Programmers do that to save memory, or to avoid the program hanging. In the old type of games, you never saw it actually happening, but we're talking cutting edge here. Everything is upfront, laid out before the players. It paradoxically adds to the aura of reality to put in reminders that what's going on is largely unreal or imaginary. Nader's locked up in the loop and he won't come out of it until you feed him a proper line of game dialogue."

"Which would be?"

"Whatever you like. But it's got to be something he can respond to, within his role in the game."

"That's tricky."

"No it isn't."

"Yes it *is*. You still haven't told me what the object of the game is."

"Okay," Geller said. "You restart him by repeating your last line. The program ignored it the first time because it didn't know it. But it has heard and learned that now, so it will recognize it the second time. If you include Nader's name, he too will know you're addressing him."

"So if I say everything twice, the program will catch on without a pause?"

"Not necessarily. But it sometimes helps, if a game-loop starts."

"All right." Pikul turned toward the store owner. "We're here, D'Arcy Nader, and that's all that matters."

Nader instantly broke out of his loop. He chuckled.

"You're right," he said. "That ist all that matters."

"What's next?" Pikul whispered to Geller.

"Get back to the plot. Why did we follow him in here?"

"Got it!" Pikul looked back at the man. "Well, Nader, you said you thought you had what we're looking for."

"I haff. Why you want it?"

"You offered it to us. Didn't you?" Pikul turned to Geller. "Didn't he?"

"He did," Geller said. She was regarding Nader with an expression of acute interest, clearly trying to fathom what was going on.

Nader said, "In which case . . . you're going to need these micropods, so you can download your new identities." He held up the gel-paks. "I assume you do both haff those industry-standard bioports you mentioned?"

"Yes," Geller said. "We've both installed bioports." But she looked a little doubtful, and said to Pikul, "We do, don't we?"

"I assume we do. I mean, here in the game. Of course, we might not." A depressing thought suddenly struck him. "If we don't, I'm not having another one inserted!"

"We'd better check," Geller said.

Nader went into memory-save mode and Geller pulled her shirt out of her jeans and turned her back toward Pikul. He took a look. Her bioport was there, although to his eye it looked slightly rougher, more puckered, more organic than it had in her nongame life.

"Yeah, it's there," he said. He told her how its appearance was a little different.

Geller grabbed his shirt and did the same for him.

"I see what you mean," she said. She turned back to Nader, who was humming the theme song again. "Yes, we both have bioports, D'Arcy Nader."

Nader jerked back into action.

"Good. Port in, and these vill tell you all you need to know for now."

Pikul and Geller inspected the gel-paks, Pikul feeling suspicious about the one he was holding. It bore the Cortical Systematics name and logo.

"What do you think?" he asked.

"Looks much the same as the one I use," Geller replied. "A miniature version of the same thing."

Nader said, "I'll leaf you two while you finish up in here. It would not be good for us all to be seen together." He smiled in a sinister way, as if this had been a significant thing to point out. He headed for the door, where he paused. "Don't do anything I wouldn't do," he said by way of departure.

He chuckled, then went out and closed the connecting door behind him.

[**13**]

"I assume that Mr. Nader is our entry point into the game," Pikul said.

"Yeah. Kind of disappointing, don't you think?"

"Who? Nader?"

"Not a well-drawn character at all. And his dialogue was only so-so."

"Yeah." Pikul considered for a moment. "'Don't do anything I wouldn't do.' That's the kind of thing you get from parents. How are we supposed to know what he would or wouldn't do?"

"In a game, you can't take anything for granted. I know what he said was banal, but maybe there's a reason for that somewhere, one we haven't come across yet. Remember, this is still just the first level."

"So do we blame ourselves for that? The bad dialogue, I mean? Would it still be bad dialogue, no matter who was ported in?"

"The game engine is obviously just getting used to us. It'll be a bit more daring, a bit more imaginative, once it warms up."

"There was one thing Nader said, about downloading our new identities. Do you know anything about that?"

"That's probably Nader-speak for moving us up to the next level of the game. Let's have a look."

She fumbled the micropod out of the gel-pak she was holding. Pikul saw it squishing floppily around her hands, like a child's balloon half filled with warm water. It never seemed to keep still, constantly swelling and deflating, rolling around in her grip. Geller managed to turn it over, where some instructions appeared on the underside.

"Oh, okay. . . that sounds straightforward enough. It says here the pods are so small they can be plugged directly into a bioport. No UmbyCord needed. Here, turn around and I'll do yours."

"Are you sure you know what you're doing, Geller?"

"Yes, and no. Yes, I'm sure I know what I'm doing, because this is just a game. No, all this is as new to me as it is to you. Nothing is real. All you have to do is relax . . . and roll with it."

"Okay, I'm rolling."

He turned away for her to attend to his bioport, and again felt her hands moving his shirt around in a way he found undeniably sexy. There was a slight pressure on his back, in the region of the bioport. Pikul wondered if his back would be flushing as much as his face, because the simple feel of her hands lightly brushing against his skin set all his nerves jangling.

But then Geller said, "Oh my God!"

"What? Oh-my-God what? What happened?"

"The whole pod disappeared into your back. Did you feel it?"

"What do you mean, *it disappeared*?"

"It kind of wriggled in. I was holding it, and then it just sucked itself in." She bent down for a closer look. A silence ensued; Pikul could hear her breathing, feel the light pressure of her breath on his back. Finally she said, "Yup, it seems to have gone right inside—"

"It disappeared into my back?!" Pikul shouted. "It's in my spine? It's worming its way around my spinal column?"

"Don't panic! It's only a game."

"Don't panic? I've got a goddamn living organism, cloned from a two-headed frog, swimming around inside me, and you say don't panic?"

"Can you feel anything?" Geller asked.

"Yes! It's the most horrible sensation—" Pikul groped around his midriff, feeling for the presence of the disgusting thing that had penetrated him. Then he stopped. "Hey, no. Now that you mention it, I can't feel a thing."

"So it's okay, then?"

"Well, I don't like the idea too much, but as far as pain goes, I've suffered a lot worse."

"Has anything happened to your vision? Are you thinking okay?"

In truth, now that he was calming down, Pikul was still thinking how irresistibly beautiful and sexy Geller looked, and how he'd like to— But this wasn't the time or place for that. It was all a game, as she kept reminding him.

"Yeah, I'm thinking okay," he said reluctantly.

"You'd better do me as well, then."

She turned away from him and with both hands raised her shirt. He looked with great pleasure at the slender curve of her bare back, the way her jeans fitted tightly over the luscious curves of her hips and buttocks. She'd lifted her shirt just high enough that he could glimpse the rounded side of one of her breasts. The bioport nestled against the flesh of her young back, closer than Pikul himself would ever dare go to her. How he dreamed of pressing himself right up against her, putting his hands on her, and—

"Get on with it!" Geller said. "What's the problem?"

"Nothing. I'm making sure I don't do anything wrong."

He sighed, then pressed the edge of the micropod against the port. Although she'd warned him it was going to happen, he was appalled at the eager speed with which the thing crawled into the narrow opening.

"It's gone," he said in a moment.

"Right inside?"

"All the way."

He touched the port with his hand. Geller did not move, although if he hadn't known her better, he would have thought she shivered with pleasurable reaction to his fingers. She stayed put, with her thin shirt seductively raised, her beautiful back virtually bare before him.

Pikul bent low and pressed his lips on her skin, right next to the bioport. Geller did not move or react. He pressed harder, opening his lips to suck and caress the firm, sleekly toned flesh of her lower back.

"What the hell are you doing?" Geller quickly stepped away and turned to face him.

Pikul straightened, looking and feeling guilty.

"Um, I don't think that was me," he said. "Not the real me. It was my game character. He took over unexpectedly. I felt it was in role. Obviously I wouldn't have done that to you. Not here, anyway."

But he was aching for her. Her eyes blazed with anger, her clothes were deliciously disarrayed.

"Don't ever do that again!" she snapped. Then she grinned, releasing the tension. "Do this instead."

She leaned forward, tilted up her lovely face and kissed him hard and passionately full on the lips.

When they disengaged from each other about a minute later, they were both flushed and panting.

"Wow!" Pikul said. "Want to show me that again?"

"Yeah, but let's think about the situation we're in."

"Who needs to think about a situation right now?"

"No, our game characters are obviously programmed to jump on each other. Wouldn't you agree?"

"Let's jump," Pikul said, trying to get his arms around her again.

"But it's only a pathetic mechanical attempt to heighten the emotional tension of the next game level."

"Okay, it's pathetic. But it's good enough for me."

"No use fighting it, is there?" Her lips were moist, her eyes were gleaming hungrily. Hungry for him.

"No," Pikul said. "But what about these new identities we have? Do you feel yours yet?"

She moved in on him again, winding one of her arms around his back and caressing his chest with her free hand.

"That sort of thing can take care of itself," she said, purring sexily.

"I'm worried about my body," Pikul said, feeling a familiar sense of panic rising in him. The same panic that struck him whenever she came so close.

"Your what? Don't worry about it."

"I mean . . . where are our actual bodies? Are they all right? What if there's danger? Are they hungry?"

"Who cares? They'll be in Kiri's chalet, where we left them. Sitting quietly, eyes closed, side by side. Like meditating."

Geller was undoing the remaining buttons on his shirt. She pushed the garment open and across his shoulders, letting it slide down from his back. She pressed herself warmly against him and started running her mouth over the skin of his chest. He could feel her lips, and the sharper indentations of her teeth.

"I don't know," Pikul said. "I feel really disembodied."

"What are you frightened of, Pikul?"

"This! No, not this! It's too much. I want you, but I keep being obsessed by reality!"

"Try this," Geller said.

She took his hand and led it to the vee of her shirt. She popped open the buttons, then pressed his hand inside and slid it slowly across her ripe young breasts. She continued to rest her fingers on his hand as he moved back and forth. Her nipples were erect and aroused, eager for his touch.

"That's what you call an embodied body," she said. "Feel how it works. The trick is not to fight the sensation when it comes."

"Yeah, you said that before. I know that sensation. I've known about it in the past."

He kissed her then, and she responded as passionately as the first time.

They ripped and pulled at each other's clothes, and by silent consent moved around behind the crates they had first sat on, where there was a shaded space on the floor. They sprawled awkwardly, but enthusiastically. Naked, they began to make serious love, strenuously, passionately, and tenderly. They cared nothing about the physical discomforts of the dirty stockroom. They were simply eager to sate the passion that had been rising in them for so long.

As they rushed to joyful climax, neither of them noticed that around them the image of the game store was beginning to melt away.

[14]

His fingers were twitching, as if his hands were still playing gently with Geller's soft and willing body, but the rest of his body was rigid and unmoving. Pikul found that he was sitting on a hard wooden bench. His legs were folded under another long bench, this one a work surface with a slow-moving conveyor belt sliding along before him from left to right. On the belt there was an endless stream of what appeared to be animal parts: tiny limbs, eyes, internal organs, bodies, tails, claws, horns. They slithered past, seeming to accuse him with their immobile state of brokenness.

Great noise burst in around him as the scene became more coherent: people's voices, grinding machinery, a crashing of something metal on something hollow, the whining of drills, distant motors, country music played over the P.A., an endless clattering and banging.

Pikul did not look down at his hands, because he

did not yet wish to discover at what they were working so expertly. Something was cool and squishy down
there. Instead he looked up and around.

He was obviously in some kind of small factory or
assembly plant. It was a large Quonset hut, with a high
arching ceiling made of corrugated iron or another
kind of sheet metal. The hut was long and narrow, built
to accommodate the lengthy, slow-moving conveyor
belt. There were dozens of dormer windows built into
the sloping walls, but without exception they'd all
been boarded up. The light that glared down on the
occupants of the hut was therefore all artificial, from
many banks of fluorescent tubes.

Pikul, thrown into this unexplained activity, was
thinking instead about Allegra Geller's lissome and
naked body, joined excitingly to his, melting into his
arms, her lips and breath hot on his face. Because it was
so recent, so immediate and personal, it was in many
ways as if she were still there with him. He knew,
though, that by some inexplicable means he was again
fully dressed, and that she was apparently no longer
anywhere around him.

He looked back at the endlessly moving conveyor
belt, its steady sideways flow and its grisly load.

The pieces of organism were sections of reptiles' or
amphibians' bodies: limbs, heads, chests, spines, hearts . . .
sometimes the pieces were as small as single eyes, claws,
or nails. The parts had been mutilated, or sectioned, so

that each body piece came with some of the nervous system attached; at least, that's what the tangles of neural tissue looked uncomfortably like to Pikul.

There were other workers on each side of him, and in other stalls beyond, stretching way up the length of the hut. By glancing surreptitiously at what they were doing, Pikul figured they must be selecting various pieces of the gruesome remains and reassembling them in some new way: overhead there was a menacing selection of small, surgical tools—scalpels, clamps, vices, and so on.

A similar range of equipment hung before him too, over his alcove. At first glance everything seemed shiny and new; only when you looked more closely did you see the tiny telltale streaks of blood.

Pikul discovered he was wearing surgical gloves and clean white clothes. A photo ID card was clipped to his shirt pocket, swinging down.

He lifted it and turned it around, so he could read what was inscribed on it.

Larry Ashen, it said. His name was Larry Ashen.

The worker in the next alcove, a long-haired man with a morose look, saw Pikul trying to read his badge. He snickered at him. Mocking Pikul, he made a play of turning his own ID card around to read it. As he did so, Pikul caught a glimpse of the man's name: it was Yevgeny Nourish.

"Hey, these cards are a pretty damn good thing!"

the man said in a deeply accented voice, the sort Pikul was starting to associate with the strangers he kept meeting. "I'm still cold Yevgeny Nourish!"

"Pleased to meet you, Mr. Nourish," Pikul said politely, remembering what Geller had said about letting the game take over. He and Nourish shook hands, their gloves squeaking as they pressed against each other.

"What is it you are doing here with us, Mr. Ashen?"

"Just finding my way, I guess."

"You haff been sent here?"

"No . . . well, maybe yes."

"Ah. I thought so. They would not tell me when I ask. I say, what is next, what should I be looking for? Give me the clue I need. Do they tell me? No, they send you and let me find out the rules all on my own."

"Yeah, I know the feeling," Pikul said. "I'm sorry."

"Are you here alone?"

"Yes. Well, at present I'm on my own, but I'm supposed—"

"And you are new here on the line?" Nourish said.

"I guess so."

"Well, let me welcome you to the Trout Farm, Mr. Ashen."

"Did you say to the *Trout Farm*?"

"Trout. You know, we are raising the baby trouts

from fertilized eggs and then stock the rivers with them." He waved his hand expansively, taking in the whole building and, presumably, much of the area beyond. Then he laughed sardonically and glanced over his shoulder as if someone might be listening. He leaned toward Pikul confidentially, his long hair hanging forward so his face was partly concealed. "Don't ask any more than this, Mr. Ashen; it's still called the Trout Farm. The entire place was being that until two, maybe three years ago. You know, these days it seems like almost every last thing used to be something else, doesn't it?"

"Yes. I guess you could say that. Nothing stands still, does it? Excuse me for a moment."

Pikul pushed his seat back and leaned over to have another look at the inside of the large hut. He was desperate to locate Geller but couldn't see her. He assumed she would still look like she used to. The photo of Larry Ashen he'd glimpsed on his ID card confirmed that his appearance hadn't changed in the transition to this new level of the game. It was a fair bet, then, that Allegra Geller would still look like Allegra Geller.

Even so, no one remotely like her was in view: everyone working in the components building looked like small-town locals, of both sexes and all ages and apparently from many different backgrounds. Tall, thin, short, stout, male, female: all the combinations except the one he sought. Fair-haired and beautiful, uniquely sexy. Allegra Geller.

Pikul slid his chair back to the bench. At once, his hands went to work.

He watched them with surprise and real interest. They were moving deftly across his workbench.

First his right hand reached down into a straw-filled box resting on the floor beside him. From this it withdrew a translucent object, premanufactured, about the size of a pita bread, made of some animal-sourced gristly matter. His hands then slit the pita thing open with a utility knife, exposing its slimy innards. While these bulged slightly, swelling out from the constraint of the gristle, his free hand selected a piece of organism from the conveyor belt: the first one Pikul saw himself picking up was a lizard-type leg, with a knee, green scales, and a horny five-fingered claw. This piece of organism was then inserted roughly into the shuddering mass, his fingers pressing it into place as if they were trying to shove a live sardine into a hard-boiled egg. When the section of the amphibian was located in position, still sticking out, his hands found a surgical needle already threaded with a coarse black yarn and they quickly sewed up the slit.

With the first one completed, his right hand started the next, reaching down for another pitalike container. This one was accomplished faster than before, with a great deal of dexterity and competence.

Yevgeny Nourish was watching suspiciously.

"You might be new at the job, Mr. Ashen," he said, "but you sure seem to know what you're doing."

"It surprises me more than it surprises you," Pikul replied with complete sincerity.

Nourish moved back to the slit-open pita case on which he himself had been working and made a couple of fumbling stitches. He was rocking back and forth in a way that reminded Pikul of the memory-save behavior of D'Arcy Nader. After a few moments Nourish looked back at him.

"You might be new at the job, Mr. Ashen," he said, "but you sure seem to know what you're doing."

Pikul was about to repeat his earlier answer, except to put more emphasis on his own sense of surprise, but then realized that this could not be the right response within the terms of the game. If he said those words again, or anything like them, Nourish would no doubt start humming the company theme.

He tried to blank his mind of his own thoughts and let himself say the first thing that occurred to him.

"I, er . . . I've been trained by the very best," he said tentatively.

"Is what I thought."

Nourish came completely out of memory-save mode and glanced around with a delicate furtiveness. He looked first along the whole length of the assembly line, then raised himself from his seat and looked across the large area behind them. He seemed satisfied no one was taking any notice of their conversation.

He leaned more closely toward Pikul.

"I was trained that way too, Larry," he said, his voice a hoarse whisper. "Listen, where is it do you plan to be eating lunch today?"

"What? I hadn't planned that far ahead yet."

The glistening gobbets of reptilian cadavers had been no inducement to hunger.

Nourish rocked back and forth. Then he glanced around with a delicate furtiveness. He looked first along the whole length of the assembly line, then raised himself from his seat and looked across the large area behind them. He seemed satisfied no one was taking any notice of their conversation.

"I was trained that way too, Larry," he said, his voice a hoarse whisper. "Listen, where is it do you plan to be eating lunch today?"

The image of food came at Pikul again. Fighting down an impulse to gag, he let the game role run within him, and from this he said, "I'm new here, as you know. I haven't made any plans for lunch yet."

"Okay, Larry. I want you to know I am recommending the Chinese restaurant in the forest here. Everybody here knows where it is. The best people in this facility always go there. All you haff to do is ask someone."

"Well, if you're thinking of going there too, maybe you and I could—"

"No, I haff other plans for lunch today," Nourish said. "It is not possible for me to be there." He looked at Pikul expectantly, clearly assuming that his meaning was clear. It was not; it merely added to Pikul's feelings of disorientation. "But you'll manage on your own. Everybody here knows where it is. The best people in this facility always go there. All you haff to do is ask someone."

"I'll do it," Pikul said earnestly. "That's where I'll eat lunch today. Chinese restaurant in the forest. Right."

"That is good," Nourish said. "Now, here is the next of what you haff to do. When you get in there, I suggest you order the special."

"I order the special," Pikul said, thinking he must have woken up in someone else's dream.

"And don't take no for an answer."

"Okay, I'll do that. The special, and don't take no for an answer. Thanks for the recommendation, Yevgeny."

"You're welcome."

Nourish returned to his tasks. He was soon working away as if Pikul did not exist.

Pikul turned back to his own bench. To his surprise, he discovered that while he and Nourish had been speaking, a long UmbyCord had uncoiled itself from some inner recess of the table and was now lying suggestively with its end close to the last pita he'd made.

What it was there for, or what he was supposed to do with it, was not at all clear. It did not appear to be doing anything at present, so he ignored it and allowed his hands to get on with their expert but mystifying tasks.

He had not been assembling long when he was interrupted by the arrival of a tall, well-built man pushing a crudely made handcart. The cart was large and square, built of canvas and metal, and was mounted on bicycle wheels with long steel spokes. A light coating of rust was working its inexorable way along the spokes and around the rims of the wheels.

The man parked the cart behind Pikul and tapped him on the shoulder.

"Larry?" he said. "Are you Larry Ashen, sir?"

"Er . . . yes!"

"They need this cart in the back room, Larry. They asked if you'd take it 'round to them."

"Me?"

"Larry Ashen, they said. Are you Larry Ashen, sir?"

"Yeah. I told you."

"They need this cart in the back room, Larry. They asked if you'd take it 'round to them."

"Okay," Pikul said. "Leave it to me."

"Special instructions. When you get there, don't take no for an answer."

"When I get where don't I take no for an answer?" Pikul said. "The back room or the restaurant?"

He was aware that next to him Nourish had stiffened in his seat and was looking across at him with a nervous expression. The tall man said, "I only work here. I get orders like everyone else."

"Okay, okay." Pikul saw that Nourish was apparently satisfied with this response. He was nodding. "I'll do it now."

The man shuffled off, leaving the cart behind him. Pikul turned to Nourish.

"Any idea what all that means?" he asked. "The back room. Where's that?"

"Out back of the assembly area," Nourish replied. "You'll find it okay. They mean they'd like you to take the cart out to them. They obviously need more motherboards for the pod assembly bays. I thought that might haff to happen. After the changes last week."

"Motherboards? Is that what these are?" Pikul glanced down and saw that a large number of the pitas, wrapped in brown wax paper, had already been stacked inside the cart. Because they hadn't been wrapped efficiently, he could glimpse dozens of scaly legs, slimy thoraxes, and disembodied eyes glistening inside. "Yes, I think they are. Motherboards. You can always tell a motherboard when you see a few of them. What do I do? Just get up and go to the back room?"

"That's it. You needn't worry about keeping up with your quota here. I haff capacity to take care of your incoming. There's no pressure on us at the moment. I can keep up. No sweat."

"Right. Thanks a lot, Yevgeny."

"You're welcome."

Pikul got up from his bench and took the handles of the cart in both hands.

Nourish leaned back and grabbed him by the arm.

"Remember, Larry," he said in a fierce, urgent whisper. "Lunch in the Chinese restaurant."

"In the forest," Pikul whispered back. "And I order the special."

"Don't take no for an answer."

"You bet I won't."

[15]

At the back of the components building there was an entrance to the pod assembly area. Pikul walked slowly down a shallow access ramp, the cart pressing its weight gently against his hands from behind. The pod assembly area was much larger than the Quonset hut he'd just left, apparently part of an older building.

The bays themselves looked like old horse stalls, hastily made over to their present use. So hastily, in fact, that piles of filthy straw were still spread on most of the dirt floor. There was a stench of horses, dung, and general animal presence. Pikul felt his nostrils tingling at the smell. It did not hang easy with the more pervasive background smell of eviscerated reptiliana: a slimy, insistent stench of river water, decaying vegetation, and cold-blooded denizens.

Each pod bay was occupied by a team of assembly workers clad in sterile protective wear, with long rubber boots and gloves, their faces swaddled in surgical masks and protective eye guards. They bent intently over their work, like teams in an operating theater.

There were obvious differences, though. Whereas an operating theater would be fanatically clean and sterile, the pod assembly bays were rancid and squalid. The workers' boots sloshed endlessly in the mud- and dung-smeared straw below the workbenches. Their every movement seemed to send up a whole new swarm of tiny flies, and their gloves and overalls were streaked with brown smears and traces of blood.

They were working on the final assembly of game-pods, clearly not dissimilar in use from the ones Pikul had seen Geller using, but a universe away in terms of quality of manufacture.

The workers here were taking the crudely made pitas that he and Yevgeny Nourish and the others had put together from the conveyor belt, and were stuffing them into fleshy, corpselike pod housings. When the new pod was full, two of the team quickly sewed it together and tossed it into a bin standing at the far side of the stall. Some of these inevitably missed, and were piling up roughly on the ground beside the bases of the bins. Some of these pitas on the floor had split open on impact. The gristly contents were spewing out in a slimy outfall of green and dark red. One of the reptilian legs appeared still to have nervous energy: it was twitching, making the electronic pita to which it had been sewn swivel endlessly in a hopeless circle.

Each pod was like a nightmare version of the real thing. Pikul was forcibly reminded by them that this was not real, this was not the world he knew. This was still a playing level of the game.

He slowly wheeled his cart past the bays, pausing at each one to deliver a number of the pitalike motherboards. In most of the bays someone accepted them from him with a dismissive grunt, or did not respond at all.

In the last bay, though, one of the masked surgeons reacted the moment he appeared at the entrance. The surgeon led Pikul to one of the farther corners of the bay, away from the mounds of split and broken pitas.

The surgeon's ID card said her name was Barb Brecken, but the photo was unmistakably that of Allegra Geller.

She slipped off her face mask.

"Hi!" she said. "How are you doing?"

"I'm real well," Pikul said, realizing as he did so that this was an exchange written into the game script.

"I saw you making contact, Larry Ashen," Geller said. "What did that guy on the assembly line say to you?"

"Can you believe any of this?" Pikul asked, forcing himself away from the droning sense of script that was in his mind. He was pleased and relieved to have located her again. "This game version of our pod? It's sick! And so unconvincing! It doesn't even look like it would work. I mean, using animal nervous systems for the electronic circuits is certainly feasible, but sewing them into those . . . those warped pita things with black thread. And they just jam the pieces in. You'd think they'd connect them up in some way first. What do you think?"

His questions ended lamely because he suddenly realized that Geller was rocking gently back and forth, humming the now familiar company theme.

When she knew he'd finished speaking, her eyes looked directly at him again.

"I saw you making contact, Larry Ashen," Geller said. "What did that guy on the assembly line say to you?"

"Sorry, Allegra!" Pikul said, then again realized he was still outside the game script. He forced himself to relax, and in a moment he felt the next line forming inescapably in his mind. Barb Brecken continued to rock back and forth while he found the words.

He resisted it, fought it, but in the end there was no more putting it off.

"He told me where to have lunch," Pikul said.

[16]

Geller and Pikul followed a ragged stream of other workers as they moved through the forest. They were walking along a gravel path that wound gently between the trees, running roughly parallel with the curving course of a small, smooth-flowing river. The sun glinted down through the high tops of the trees, throwing fitful shadows across the faces of everyone passing below. From time to time the surface was broken by a fish leaping to claim a fly hovering above the water. It was warm and peaceful. Pikul thought it would have presented an idyllic scene if not for the known purpose of the buildings they had just left, and the unknown purpose of the building toward which they were now going.

The game plan at this level did not appear to provide dialogue for them, so although Pikul was anxious to discuss events with Geller, he said nothing. Instead, they held hands and walked along quietly, savoring the fresh smell of the trees, the warm sunlight, and the sounds of the river. They were not alone in their silence.

Soon they saw a building in a clearing ahead of them. It was an ordinary Victorian red-brick farmhouse, standing amidst the trees. Nothing about it suggested Chinese connections, other than a sign that had been planted on the lawn in front of the building:

Mona Zhang's Beijing Cuisine

Still continuing to follow the trickle of other lunching workers, Geller and Pikul walked across the lawn and past this sign. They went inside.

Soon they were sitting at a round, Formica-covered table. At its center was a lazy Susan serving wheel. Various small platters of samples and appetizers were resting in the compartments of the wheel.

Pikul glanced around at the interior of the restaurant.

Most, but not all, of the other tables were occupied by their fellow workers. There were still plenty of vacant spots, should others arrive later. The mood in the place could not be described as cheerful: many of the people were sitting around in sullen, suspicious silence. A restaurant dog, a mongrel with a great deal of heavy, collielike fur, was basking in the corner of the large room, taking in the warmth from a pane of sunlight.

The silence that had fallen as they entered the restaurant hung around them, making Pikul apprehensive. Geller, however, stayed calm, at least on the surface. She sat elegantly at the table, her hands resting lightly on the shiny surface. Pikul glanced around at the other diners, sensing in some horrible but incomprehensible way that he already knew many of the people around him. How could this be? They were only figments of the imagination.

To his relief, the fact that he was staring back at them seemed to have the desired effect, and within a few moments a semblance of normality had returned to the restaurant.

After a few minutes a waiter approached their table. He was a young, athletic Chinese, wearing a white jacket and neatly pressed dark trousers. He was carrying a tray with rice and tea.

"We have a nice fresh sea bass today," he said, placing everything down on the table. "Shall I bring it for you?"

Geller glanced first at Pikul, then to the waiter, and shrugged in agreement.

Pikul, though, raised himself slightly in his seat and looked the waiter in the eye.

"No," he said. "We will both have the special."

The waiter looked stunned. It seemed to Pikul that a chill wave of reaction flowed across the other diners in the restaurant. Many of them were looking across the room toward their table.

The waiter had started to rock back and forth, and was pursing his lips, presumably preparing himself for a burst of corporate humming.

"Did you hear me, Chinese waiter?" Pikul said firmly. "We want the special. We—want—the—special."

The waiter unlocked, and blinked.

"The special is for, ah, special occasions," he said. "I am not able to bring you the special."

"I'm not taking no for an answer."

"The special is for, ah, special occasions," the waiter said again. "I cannot bring you the special."

"But this *is* a special occasion," Pikul said. "It's . . . I mean, it's . . . " He waited for inspiration, believing that the game script must be there to help him out. Geller was watching him with amused curiosity. "It's . . . her *birthday!*" he finally got out, waving his hand in an explanatory fashion toward Geller. "Yes, it's her birthday today."

The waiter locked up again for a few moments, but then unfroze.

"A birthday is indeed a special occasion," he said. "I will therefore bring you the special."

He walked away toward the serving door.

"And make it snappy!" Pikul called after him.

The waiter paused, then turned and bowed slightly.

"You will certainly find it . . . snappy, sir," he said.

↔   ↔   ↔

"I guess the special isn't popular," Pikul observed to Geller.

"I guess not."

"But you know, really, don't you?" he said to her, looking insistently into her eyes. "You don't have to guess about what's going on here, like me. I mean, you built all this into the game when you invented the system. It's your game, your private universe."

"That's where you're wrong, Pikul. I don't know what's happening here, any more than you do. It's one of the principal features of *eXistenZ* that you still have to learn and appreciate. You have to find out what it really is, what the game creates. Anything is possible once you start playing, and it's outside the control of the code of the game. The code of the game simply does not contain it."

"So you're telling me, just for a simple example, that as of this moment you don't know what the special is going to be?"

"Correct. I don't."

"Or why we ordered it?" Pikul went on.

"I do know that, as it happens. We ordered the special because another game character told you to order it. *eXistenZ* is a character-led game. What the players do is imagine a number of parameters, based on their unconscious wishes, their experiences, their memories, sometimes they're based on their deliberate desires. The characters we meet in the game are a part of this process: they might be people we've heard of, or would like to meet, or people we once knew long ago in our real lives and have forgotten about. They can even be historical characters. Sometimes the characters in the game are the other people you've ported into the game alongside. At the moment, for instance, you are clearly imagining me and I'm imagining you, so we both exist in the game. *eXistenZ*, you see. The characters predominate, though. It's as simple as that. If one of them tells us something, or gives us a task to perform, then that is the direction the script of the game will be taking. It's a clue we can't ignore. But that's basic game-playing."

"I want to put the game on pause," Pikul said. Geller looked at him in surprise. "The game can be paused, can't it?" he said. "I mean, all games can be paused. That's right, isn't it?"

"Yeah, of course. But why do that? Why stop it now, when it's just starting to get interesting? Aren't you dying to find out what's special about the special?"

Pikul fidgeted with the lazy Susan, rotating it with his fingers. Tempting snacks made of golden batter and noodles and dim sum went circling slowly past.

"Look, I have nothing against the game," he said. "It's just that I'm starting to feel a bit disconnected from my real life. I'm kind of losing touch with the texture of it. You know what I mean? I actually think there's an element of psychosis involved in this sort of game. I mean, I no longer know where my body really is, or where reality is . . . or what I've actually done, or not done. These things can be pretty important, you know."

Geller selected a dim sum as it circled past her, and examined it in her fingertips before putting it in her mouth. She chewed it contemplatively.

"What you're saying is a good sign, Pikul," she said. "I mean, it's a good sign in terms of you appreciating the game. It means your nervous system is fully engaging with the game architecture. The game is a lot more fun to play when it starts to feel realer than real."

"Yeah, let the fun begin," Pikul said.

He pushed back his chair and stood up. He took a deep breath, then screamed at the top of his lungs.

"*eXistenZ* is paused!" he yelled, making the cutlery on the next table rattle in reaction. "The game is on hold! *eXistenZ* stops right here!"

The other diners all turned to stare at him in surprise. But by then the Chinese restaurant was already melting away.

[**17**]

Pikul was sitting on a bed with a beautiful woman who was smiling up at him from where she sprawled across the covers. He thought gloomily, If that's not Allegra Geller, I'm dreaming. Then he thought, If I'm not dreaming, then I'm dead and I've gone to Heaven.

It was . . . and so he wasn't and he hadn't.

The walls of the guest cabin at Kiri Vinokur's ski club gradually solidified around them, revealing and outlining a tangibly real Geller lying an intimately short distance away from him, connected to him by an equally substantial-looking UmbyCord. Her MetaFlesh game-pod lay between them amid the kicked-up humps of the brightly colored covers of the bed.

Pikul tried to speak but made only a liquid bur-bling noise. He waited, watching reality reform. When it seemed complete, he tried again.

"Did I do that?" he said.

"Did you stop the game, you mean? I think you did."

"Wow," he said with conviction, if not with a great deal of subtlety.

"So how does it feel?" Geller said to him, smiling.

"How does what feel?"

"Your real life . . . the one that was so important for you to come back for."

"Sitting here with you on a bed feels completely unreal. For any number of reasons."

"So that wasn't what you wanted." She shifted position, straightened the untidy bedcovers, laid the game-pod more in the center of the space between them. "And reality in general? How does that feel?"

"Pretty good. I'm sure you knew that was going to happen."

"I suspected that pausing the game like that would bring us back here to the ski lodge. But you're stuck now, aren't you? You've got what you wanted, what you thought you wanted. But you also want to go back to the Chinese restaurant because something engrossing was happening there. You didn't know what it was, but it was at least something interesting. Here . . . there's nothing happening. We're safe here, but safety is ultimately boring."

"Geller . . . what's that you're chewing?"

She worked her jaw a couple more times, and ran

her tongue over her teeth. "Is it bothering you?"

"No. What is it you're eating?"

"I don't know. Something spicy."

"Is it dim sum?"

She swallowed quickly, clearing her mouth. "No. Not dim sum."

"Are you sure?"

"Sure I'm sure. What are you implying, Pikul?"

"I'm having trouble with all this," he said. "Reality doesn't feel so real anymore. I'm not sure that here, where we are now, is real at all. As far as I'm concerned *this also* feels like a game. Sitting here on a bed with the most beautiful woman I've ever met." He looked away from her for a moment, thinking hard. Then he said, "Did we really make love together?"

Her reaction was instant. "Definitely not!"

The sharpness of her tone surprised him.

"At least that much is clear," he said. "At least as far as you're concerned. You're not in any doubt."

"Why do you ask?"

"Because it feels to me as if we did," Pikul said. "I have extremely clear memories of doing it, of liking it, and of wanting a whole lot more of it. You seemed to feel the same way. At the time, I mean."

"No . . . our game characters had sex with each other. That's the sort of thing that happens inside *eXistenZ*. But it wasn't real, it doesn't mean anything. Don't make assumptions about you and me based only on that. Things would be different if we were to do it together for real."

Pikul thought about that for the moment. She had said, *if* we were to do it for real . . . while to him it felt as if they already had.

"I'm actually just like that," he said after a while. "I mean, the game character who made love to you . . . he's *exactly* like me. If you liked what happened with the game character . . . well, I want you to know you got the real Ted Pikul in there, in the game store."

"Before you get any more ideas up and running, I can assure you that you didn't get the real Allegra Geller there. I mean the game character didn't."

"What makes you say that?"

She stretched over, raising her face to his, and kissed him gently but affectionately.

"In real life I tend to lose control. It can get seriously messy." She allowed him to return her kiss, and for a few moments Pikul thought she was about to give him a seriously messy time. But then she added, "Come on . . . let's port in and go back to the game."

"Aw . . . not yet."

"We can't leave the game where we did. It was about to get interesting."

"Okay, but afterward?"

"Afterward is what we do next. That's a promise, or maybe even a warning."

"All right," he said, and grinned happily at her. He reached down to the game-pod and flicked the Play nipple.

The room began to dissolve away from them.

[18]

The Chinese restaurant quickly reformed around them, with light and noise and movement swimming into life.

The lazy Susan was still revolving slowly after Pikul had propelled it with his hand. Geller continued to chew her dim sum. As she swallowed the remains of it, the waiter approached their table bearing a large tray of dishes. He set them down proudly on the lazy Susan.

"Special order for the birthday girl," he said. "Enjoy your meal."

Pikul and Geller stared at the dishes.

Each one contained an assortment of cooked reptiles and amphibians: frogs with bamboo shoots; deep-fried lizards in sesame seeds; a huge toad set upright amidst stuffed mushrooms, with a couple of pieces of corn pushed into his eye sockets; a soup thick with noodles and boiled newts; slices of roast snake with oyster sauce. The lazy Susan slowly drifted round and round, bearing this bizarre but strangely beautiful feast before them.

"My God," Geller said.

"You take the words right out of my mouth."

A single saucer-shaped bowl had a compartment to itself, and as it moved on toward Geller, Pikul pointed it out.

"Recognize a friend?" he said.

Geller took a closer look: it was the two-headed salamander that had ridden on the truck with them from the gas station.

Pikul gulped. "Two heads and six legs," he said. "I think I've lost my appetite."

The waiter was still hovering beside their table.

"Not hungry anymore?" he said. "Great shame, great pity. Mutant reptiles and amphibians provide new and previously unimagined taste sensations. Secret Oriental recipes."

"Well, yeah," Geller said. "Thanks, but no thanks. No offense, mind."

"Shall I clear all this away?" the waiter said.

Pikul caught the glimmer of expression that had passed over Geller's face. She was indicating: this is the special, this is something special, a game character told us to choose it.

"No, it looks terrific," Pikul said decisively. He

glanced back at Geller, who was nodding slowly. "Thank you. We're happy."

"Very good," the waiter replied. "Enjoy."

This time he walked away, holding his tray at his side.

Pikul looked thoughtfully at the array of animals lying before him, then reached out and selected the toad with mushrooms. He scooped the toad onto his plate, but returned the mushrooms to the lazy Susan.

With precise movements he began breaking the toad's muscular limbs off and stripping away the meat.

"Pikul, what are you doing?"

"I don't know." He'd bitten into the side of the toad, feeling the flesh spreading as his jaw clamped down on it, and the bones of the animal's skeleton breaking and separating. His mouth filled with the oily, meaty flavor of meat. "I find it disgusting, but I can't help myself!"

"That's great!" Geller wrinkled her nose in disdain at him. "You can't help yourself."

"This isn't my choice," he said with his mouth full. He swallowed, then took another bite. This time he took a leg. After he'd chewed on it a few times he turned the limb around with his fingers, then stripped the soft meat from the bone by pulling against his teeth.

He looked up from what he was doing. He had

now dismembered the toad, with many of its largest bones lying on his plate. He set to work on the deep-fried lizards, scraping off the sesame seeds, pulling away the stringy flesh and laying out the tiny bones on his plate. Everything was stir-fried to perfection: the meat fell neatly from the bones.

Pikul's fingers were slimy and gobbets of melted fat were dripping from the ends. As before, when he'd been sitting by the conveyor belt, his hands carried on their work of their own volition.

"I'm interested in what you're doing," Geller said when he seemed to be flagging.

"Interested?" Pikul said, glancing down with horror at what he was doing. "You think this is interesting?"

"Yeah, it's fascinating to watch," Geller said. "It's a genuine game urge, obviously something your game character, Larry Ashen, was born to do and is good at. Don't fight it."

"Actually, I did start out by fighting it. But it didn't do me any good, so I'm just rolling with it for the moment."

As he spoke his hands were snapping one of the toad's long thigh bones and twisting a strip of frog-sinew around it to form an angled piece. He and Geller watched with horrid fascination as his hands quickly pushed all the various pieces together, slotting them in with shreds of skin, gristle, and sinews to hold them in place, and using the amphibians' own joints to form swivels and cogs and other moving parts.

The grotesquely twinned neckbone of the six-legged salamander was the last piece to be put into place. It seated itself neatly with a distinct click, and as Pikul held up the assembly, it was clear that the necks had formed the mechanism of a trigger.

He was holding a cadaver-gun almost identical to the one that had been used in the assassination attempt at the church.

"Oh my God!" Pikul said in a voice full of awe. "This looks awfully familiar. Are you sure this is okay?"

Geller was looking as uncomfortable as he felt.

"It should be okay," she said, but she didn't sound at all sure.

While his right hand held the gun, Pikul's left hand suddenly moved. Smeared with grease and fragments of meat, it went into his mouth. He sensed a brief, horrifying taste of spicy meat tormenting his tastebuds, and felt his own fingers pulling and twisting at his teeth.

When the hand withdrew, it was holding a bridge of three teeth, one of them bearing a gold filling.

He loaded the teeth efficiently into the magazine of the new cadaver-gun. Bizarre objections to the cadaver-gun flashed through Pikul's mind, about caliber and rifling and explosive power, but he had already seen how well the guns worked. He was in no mood to argue with his own hands.

"Is that your bridge?" Geller said, of the false teeth.

"You saw where the teeth came from."

"I meant, do you wear a bridge in real life?"

"Absolutely not. My real teeth are perfect. Don't ask me how I knew that thing was in my mouth."

"It probably wasn't," Geller said dryly, "until you ordered the special."

Pikul held the stock of the grotesque gun, and with a practiced motion slapped the magazine into the handle. He pulled the slide back and released it, and with a horrible sinister clicking noise one of the teeth snapped out of the bridge and moved precisely into the chamber.

Smiling devilishly, Pikul pointed the weapon at Geller.

"Death to the vile demoness Allegra Geller!" he said, and waggled his eyebrows at her mock-threateningly.

She slid her chair back in alarm. It scraped across the floor with a loud screeching sound. Her eyes were wide with fear.

"Hey, that's not funny!" she shouted.

"I don't mean it," he said.

"I do. Put the goddamn gun down!"

He saw the real terror persisting in her eyes, so he lowered the gun at once. He shook his head in disbelief at what he'd done. Geller had gone pale, but without looking at him she moved her chair back so she was able to sit against the edge of the table once more. Her hands were trembling.

Pikul took all this in, filled with regret. Even so, his hand still held on to the cadaver-gun.

"I'm sorry," he said to her. "I couldn't resist that, somehow."

"For a moment, I thought—I really thought you were going to do it."

He shook his head. "Not you. I wouldn't kill you. But you know, I really do feel an incredible urge to kill someone here. That's what my script role is in the game. I'm an assassin."

Geller gripped the edge of her bowl of newt soup, presumably the closest thing she had to a defensive weapon. Quite an effective one, Pikul instantly realized when he looked at what was in it. He didn't relish the idea of having a dozen hot dead newts thrown in his face.

"You're not the target," he said. "Relax."

"Then who is it?"

"I need to kill our friend the waiter."

"Okay, that makes sense. I'll call him." Geller turned around in her chair and waved a hand. "Waiter! Waiter!"

"Do you mean that?" Pikul said. "You want me to go ahead?"

"If it's in the game, just do it. Don't hesitate even for a moment."

"But everything feels so realistic. I don't usually go around killing people. I don't think I really could go through with it."

"You won't be able to stop yourself. You might as well find out what it feels like, and enjoy it."

"Free will is obviously not a factor in this little game world of yours," Pikul observed.

"It's exactly like real life," Geller said. "There's just enough free will to make things interesting. Anyway, it's not my world. It's ours."

"So you keep saying."

Pikul spotted the waiter making his way toward them, weaving between the tables. He was wearing an expectant smile on his face. Other diners were trying to summon him to their tables, but he ignored them all. His expression evinced a total desire to please Pikul and Geller.

"Shit, he's smiling," Pikul said quietly.

"So what?"

"So I find him nice. What's he ever done to me? I'm not going to go through with it."

"You don't have much choice," Geller said. "Free will is restricted here. Remember?"

The waiter arrived at their table, holding his order pad expectantly.

↔   ↔   ↔

"How may I help you?" the waiter said.

"Well, for a start you could quit smiling."

"I'm sorry if I am causing offense, sir. But it is my job to make your lunch as pleasant as possible."

"I don't want you being nice, you hear?" Pikul lifted the gun up from the table and pointed it at the waiter. He tightened his finger on the trigger. "I found this in my soup, and I'm upset about it."

"I can only apolo—"

But Pikul fired!

There was a loud bang and the gun recoiled. The tooth-bullet slammed into the waiter's face, right under his eye. A chunk of his cheekbone flew away in a spray of blood, and the man's head jerked like that of a prizefighter punched in the face.

The waiter staggered back, dropping his pad and pressing his hands to his face. His white jacket was already scarlet with blood, which was pumping out of him at a horrific rate. He collided with another table, stumbled, seemed about to collapse on the floor, but then recovered.

His face had been transformed into a hideous mask of bloodied anger. He lurched back toward their table, and as he did so he produced a long meat cleaver from under his jacket.

Geller snatched up the bowl of hot newt soup she'd been toying with and with both hands threw it in the waiter's face. The steaming liquid, and all the newts, flooded over his face and shoulders. He screamed in agony, plucking desperately at the newts and the soft noodles, trying to wipe the sticky soup liquid out of his eyes. One newt was clinging stubbornly to the horrific bleeding cavity where his cheekbone had been.

Geller's action delayed him for only a couple of seconds.

He came at them again, the cleaver raised above his head. Before either of them could dodge away, he brought the chopping knife down with horrific strength and muscular agility. It smashed against the cadaver-gun in Pikul's hand, slicing off a tiny part of the tip of the muzzle, then collided with the edge of the Formica tabletop. It made a metallic ringing sound as it bounced away.

The gun began to bleed.

The waiter collapsed forward across the table, bashing into the lazy Susan and throwing the contents of the remaining dishes all over the floor.

He was still gripping the cleaver, and now he turned to Pikul, grappling with deadly menace across the ruined tabletop toward him. Blood was pumping from the injury in his shattered cheekbone. Noodles and dead newts were splattered on his hair and face.

Before the waiter could lever himself upright,

Pikul shot him again. He fired the gun straight down the waiter's open mouth.

A segment of the Chinese man's skull blew out of the back of his head and skimmed across the tabletop like a tiny Frisbee. It landed, spinning. Pikul saw that a gold-capped tooth was buried in the bone.

The gun was bleeding heavily and covering his hand in gore. Pikul threw it aside in disgust.

Unseen by Geller or Pikul, the restaurant dog had left his spot in the sunlight and was now cowering close to their table. As the cadaver-gun landed on the floor and skittered across the polished boards, the dog leaped out from its position and took the gun in his jaws. He loped off with it to a nearby table and crouched down underneath, between the diners' legs.

He began to gnaw at the gun, growling.

A tense stillness had spread across the entire restaurant. All the other diners were staring in horror toward their table; some were taking cover, ducking down as well as they could in the confined spaces. Pikul stood up slowly, feeling shaky but nonetheless determined to reassure the other people.

"It's all right," he said loudly to everyone within earshot. "Just a little misunderstanding over the check. Er . . . it's all okay. Pay no attention and enjoy your meal."

After a few more uncomfortable moments, the

other diners turned back to their meals with an air of sinister reluctance. Those who had ducked to avoid being caught in the cross fire stood upright, looking embarrassed, then sat back down in their chairs and picked up their chopsticks.

Pikul looked around in confusion at the strangely inactive room. A wild fear was running through him.

"What do you think, Pikul?" Geller said.

"I think I feel a serious game-urge coming on me. I'm out of control. Let's get out of here!"

He took her hand.

A movement on the far side of the room was pulling at his attention. There were two glass portholes in the white-painted metal serving doors leading to the kitchen, and through one of these Pikul had seen a man in a chef's hat. He was beckoning urgently to them.

"We can get out through the kitchen!" Pikul called to Geller. "That way!"

They zigzagged between the tables, inadvertently knocking against several of them in their haste. They barged their way through the serving doors.

They found themselves in a large professional kitchen, all gleaming aluminum surfaces, huge ranges of gas burners, row upon row of overhead racks from which shimmering steel pans hung in long lines. Flames and steam rose from where an intent group of white-coated workers were cooking busily on the far side of the room, but everywhere kitchen staff were dashing around in the familiar apparent confusion of a busy kitchen. Pans and appliances constantly clattered, and chefs and their assistants bellowed a stream of orders across the bowed heads of the more humble staff.

On many shelves and polished working surfaces lay the ingredients of the meals. Legs, claws, abdomens, heads of reptiles were scattered everywhere, some piled into heaps on huge serving plates, others arrayed neatly on chopping blocks for the attention of the *sous*-chefs.

A huge glass-sided tank had been placed against the wall at one side, and in the murky green water dozens of dark, reptilian shapes constantly moved. The surface of the tank shifted and heaved like turbid oil.

One large creature, apparently a hideous mutant between toad and snake, pressed itself against the glass with suckered feet splayed out. Its belly was pale and vulnerable. Its head, prodding up above the surface of the water, surged slowly from side to side, a long pink tongue reaching endlessly around it. Its body breathed convulsively as it sucked in air with a desperate jerkiness.

Pikul's precipitate entry into the kitchen had startled several of the workers close to the door, and now a wave of reaction spread through the room. Faces stared at him and Geller from all sides.

Moving swiftly, the chef who had waved at them stepped forward from where he'd been concealed by the doors swinging open.

It was Yevgeny Nourish.

"How did you enjoy the meal I am preparing for you?" he said cheerfully. He was holding the eviscerated remains of a large lizard.

"It was . . . revealing," Pikul said, trying not to recoil in surprise at seeing the man there.

"Yes," Geller said. "Not what we expected at all."

"Well, no matter what you haff thought of it," Nourish said. "You both passed our little test with flying colors."

"It was a *test?*" Geller said.

"What else?"

"If it was only a test, why was it important enough to make the Chinese waiter die?" she said.

"You know how it is with waiters," Nourish said, tapping the side of his nose with his finger. "Waiters are hearing many things being said around them. People let their guard slip when they are eating. They are relaxed, they are saying things that perhaps they shouldn't. Restaurants haff traditionally been used by spies for centuries, for the gaining background information. This restaurant in particular is notorious: it has many people, it is full of people, who used to be working for other game companies, and others who will probably be changing jobs in the near future. A waiter is having many opportunities for listening in, eaves-dropping you say, and in consequence it is passing on information he can do to those who might be paying him."

"Are you saying he betrayed you?" Pikul asked.

"He has betrayed all of us." Nourish stepped back to where there was a bar-locked emergency exit door. He pushed it open with a loud clanging noise from the bar. "Now, out this way! Quickly!"

[19]

The door opened directly into the woods. A short path led down through the trees to the river, where a second path followed the bank.

The three of them walked quickly along this, while Nourish calmly pointed out the various dams, vats, and breeding pools that had been built across or in the water. He seemed oblivious of the scene of carnage they had left behind them in the restaurant, and instead serenely showed them the insemination terraces, the breeding pools, the growth extension sections, and finally the sorting pans, where individual species were channeled off prior to final dispatch either to the restaurant or to the assembly building.

All the various areas of the Trout Farm were teeming with mutilated, mutated life, scrabbling in the shallow water as if desperate to escape. Dark, malign shapes moved horribly just beneath the surface, and in the growth extension and sorting areas the surface of the water was constantly being broken as the frantic amphibians either grabbed air or tried to find some way out of the watery hell into which they'd been born.

Some of the beings were not able to survive, and their bodies drifted to the sides of the vats or up against the banks of the river itself. From their appearance, these creatures were dysfunctional, bred not for survival or evolutionary credibility, but for their individual organs or limbs. Even some of the living ones were so malformed they could only swim belly up, paddling desperately in the muddy water to try to move around and breathe. Others, making it somehow to the edges, would roll over onto their sides, their distorted limbs flailing helplessly and their protruding eyes goggling at the sky.

"Is this where you come and collect the ingredients for the day's special?" Pikul said.

"No . . . this is being the development area. We don't cull from here. What we are doing is coming to development for ideas. You never know what you might be finding here, and what ideas they might be sparking off for new types of weapons. There's always an element of chance in the animals you are finding in this stretch of the river. We generally are using only successful mutants, but you never know when something might be coming in handy for a specialized piece of equipment. Before we decide what use it is we are going to put them to, we are transferring them first to the tank in the kitchen."

"And they're all eaten?"

"By no means. Some are being eaten of course, but many are being used in other ways." Nourish gave a harsh, sardonic laugh at the look of disgust Pikul could feel on his own features and see on Geller's. "We originally are starting to raise reptilian mutants for their nervous systems. These were the basis of the main logic engines in the game-pods. But then we are finding quite by chance that some of the reptiles were rather tasty, especially when they are being fried quickly in the Chinese style. Once we had established this, and we are realizing we already had a number of Chinese people working for us, we opened the Chinese restaurant as a cover for our other activities.

"Of course," he went on, "our main interest is in using the animals as components for undetectable and hypoallergenic weapons. There is not a defensive security system in the world that is picking out our handguns, grenades, antipersonnel mines, and so on. We are taking our feelings right up to the feet of our enemies, so to speak. And speaking of our enemies, it's important that the two of you are going back to work at Cortical Systematics. We are needing to maintain as many active agents in there as we can. There's an unholy mess in the restaurant that you helped make, but I can take care of all that. No worries."

"Agents?" Pikul said.

"Agents."

Pikul thought about this as they walked along.

"The Trout Farm is owned by Cortical Systematics?" Geller asked.

"Yes." He grimaced bitterly. "Their corporate slogan is ought to be: 'Enemies of Reality.'"

Maybe it was the use of the word "corporate," or more simply an overload of recent horrible events, but a certain light-headedness suddenly swum over Pikul. He felt the first chords of the Antenna corporate theme sounding in his mind, like a private jukebox starting a new track. Resisting the urge to start humming along with it, he allowed a game role to take over again.

"Reality is a fragile thing," he said tonelessly. It was extraordinary to feel these words and sentences forming of their own accord inside his mind. "Most people think that reality must of course be the most solid thing, but it frequently is not. Inner reality, emotional reality, imagined reality . . . all these are as plausible as external or objective reality. Anyway, what is reality without someone to observe or measure it? Reality in all its forms is being threatened now, more than ever. It is being eroded and it is washing away in the deforming storm of nonreality, which masquerades as reality and which will eventually replace it if we do not take the appropriate steps. Nonreality is deformed and crippled and limping and hideous and pathetic, threatening to engulf us all."

Geller was staring at him in admiring disbelief.

"Wow!" she said.

"You like that?"

"Where did it come from?"

"The game made me do it," he said modestly.

"I'm impressed."

Nourish also appeared to be impressed. Smiling broadly, he lunged at Pikul and gave him a great bear hug. Then he turned to Geller and did the same.

"That proves you have become trustworthy Realists," Nourish said warmly. "We love you for that. Welcome aboard." He raised his hand in farewell. "Now I must leave you, but I'll be back. We'll be in touch. Have a nice day."

He turned around and with one more friendly wave began walking back toward the restaurant.

Pikul and Geller resumed their stroll. Pikul felt the glow of pride starting to recede from him.

"What did he mean just now, about enemies?" he said. "Enemies of what? Reality?"

"That's what it sounded like to me."

Pikul silently agreed. He realized he was being drawn into something yet again.

"Or did he really mean, enemies of *eXistenZ?*" he said. "I'm trying to work this out. Who are the Realists? Assuming they have a game role, are they the game-world equivalent of the Anti-eXistenZialists, the people in the real world who were trying to kill you—"

"I wouldn't take it too seriously," Geller said.

"—who presumably still are trying desperately to kill you?" Pikul went on.

"Well, I don't know."

"Of course, you never seem to take this kind of thing seriously. But maybe you should." Pikul stared around at the placid woods with the sun streaming down through the leaves and branches, then looked at the turbulent, churning waters of the Trout Farm where the thousands of mutant reptiles scrambled to escape their horrific fate. It was a scene of sylvan peace and calm, yet also one of unimaginable horrors. "Why does the name Cortical Systematics seem so familiar?"

"You feel that too? I've been trying to remember."

"We saw it somewhere."

Geller touched a long finger to her forehead as she stared thoughtfully at the ground. A lizard skittered away across the path.

"At the game store!" she said. "We saw it everywhere in D'Arcy Nader's game store. Do you remember?"

"Yes," Pikul said. "So that would make it . . . what? The game-world equivalent of our own company? Cortical Systematics would therefore be the virtual-reality version of Antenna Research."

"'Only from Cortical Systematics,'" Geller intoned ironically. "I wonder what their company theme sounds like?"

Pikul frowned. "So what's next?" he said. "Do we go meekly back to work in the assembly building and say nothing?"

"I guess so."

"It sounds as though Nourish and his Realists are preparing to sabotage the Trout Farm. Before you know it they'll be planning to assassinate game designers."

They were still walking along the riverbank, leaving the turmoil of the Trout Farm well behind them. Here it was genuinely peaceful again in the sunlit forest, with just the sounds of the river and the occasional calls of songbirds high in the branches above them.

"I don't feel threatened by the thought of those fanatics, you know," Geller said. "Maybe I should, but—"

"I didn't mean—"

"It's okay. We're just game characters in here. It's wrong to mix up our real-life loyalties with the game or you'll lose for sure."

"Lose?"

"The game," she said. "It's what we're still doing. Playing a game."

"All right," he said. "So what do we do next?"

[20]

Reality dissolved, reality firmed up again. Trees faded away, walls blocked themselves in. The sunlit sky went dark, a grimy ceiling plastered with ancient posters of Darth Vader and Indiana Jones obtruded itself. The sounds of the river died down, replaced by a jangling electronic racket, mixed with pop music, which flooded the room.

Pikul found himself leaning forward, looking closely at a Cortical Systematics corporate logo. It was printed on a game-pak.

Geller was beside him. He nudged her to point out that the name had appeared again, but she was looking away, across the room. Pikul followed her stare. They had reappeared in D'Arcy Nader's Game Emporium, haunt of Geller's youth, and were squeezed into an aisle between the racks of games, surrounded by many other customers.

Geller looked back at him. "Do you recognize where we are?" she asked.

"Yes, of course. Do you see Nader anywhere?"

"Not yet."

She pushed her way along the aisle toward the raised counter where the cash register was situated. Pikul followed.

The cashier was the same sallow young man they'd seen before. He was sitting at the counter, writing on a pad of paper in front of him. His sour expression hadn't improved.

Geller said to him, "We're looking for D'Arcy Nader. Is he here?"

The cashier made no response. He continued to write. The lenses of his spectacles were grimy and covered in white flecks, Pikul noticed, and he was wearing a name tag.

"Try using his name," he prompted Geller.

"I was about to," she said. "Hugo Carlaw, is D'Arcy Nader here?"

The young man cashier looked down at them, then scanned the store and locked the cash register.

"Yes," he said. "Mr. Nader is most certainly here."

"May we see him?" Geller asked.

"He won't talk to you."

"He did the last time we were here."

"Things have changed since then. You surely know why."

"No," Pikul said. "We don't. We would still like to see him."

"Suit yourself," Hugo Carlaw said. He stood up and came down from the raised counter. "Come with me. I think he's in the stockroom out back."

Carlaw moved into the main body of the store. Customers still thronged the aisles, taking no notice of him. They passed down one of the wider aisles toward the door at the back of the store, and as Pikul and Geller followed the taller Carlaw, Pikul had the impression that everyone was looking intently at them. It was only an impression, though: whenever he turned toward anyone and looked directly at them, they averted their gaze.

They followed Carlaw to the grimy door they knew led to the stockroom. Carlaw pushed it open. It was dark inside and there was a sweet, sickly smell in the air.

Carlaw closed the door, and the darkness was complete.

"You recognize that smell?" he asked.

"What are you doing?" Geller said. "Turn on the light."

"Sure, I'll turn on the light. When I do, you'll see for yourself what makes that smell. I just thought you'd like the information broken to you gently."

Pikul said, "What information—"

But then Carlaw turned on the light.

They were in the familiar, crowded stockroom, and the two crates they'd sat on earlier were still in place. But between them—

"You want to see Nader," Carlaw said. "There he is."

Nader was lying on the floor in a terrible, contorted shape. His legs were twisted unnaturally beneath his body, and his head was thrown back at a horrible angle. They could see his face: his eyes were bulging open sightlessly, and his skin was a deep, unnatural purple.

The hideous color was eerily matched by the veiny purple streaks in the UmbyCord wrapped tightly around his neck.

"My God!" Pikul said, shocked.

"What happened?" Geller said hoarsely.

Carlaw looked at them with a sardonic expression, as if implying that they should already know. Then he turned away and began rummaging around on one of the shelves behind him. When he had found what he was looking for, he turned back.

He was pointing a cadaver-gun at them.

It was instantly, horribly familiar to Pikul. It was the one he'd constructed in the Chinese restaurant, the one he'd used on the waiter. The end of the barrel was neatly sliced off, and there were signs of teeth marks around the rest of the gun.

Dog teeth.

↔   ↔   ↔

Carlaw hefted the cadaver-gun in his hand. "You, Mr. Pikul, should not have killed the Chinese waiter."

"Why not?" Pikul said defensively. "It was in the game script, I felt it was a game role."

"He was your contact at the Trout Farm," Carlaw said, looking at him as if he was stupid. "He was a damn good man. One of the best." He stared thoughtfully at the weapon, and again weighed it in his hand. "His dog brought me this."

"But we had another contact there," Pikul said, defending his actions, which he felt were under attack by this unpleasant young man.

"Who was that?"

"Yevgeny Nourish," Pikul replied. "He seemed to know exactly who we were."

"He did. That's because D'Arcy Nader tipped him off you were coming. Nader had it all worked out because he was a mole for Cortical Systematics."

"I'm not getting this," Pikul said, genuinely confused. "Who was he working for?"

"Who? Nader or Nourish?"

"Both of them. Who matters more?"

"To you, the only one who mattered was the waiter. He was your contact, not Nourish."

"Then who was Yevgeny Nourish?" Pikul said, by now completely lost.

"I think I know what it is," Geller said. She'd been

slowly easing herself to one side, putting distance between Pikul and herself. Pikul briefly wondered if this was preparatory for an attack on Carlaw, or was it so she might escape if Carlaw was to open fire? The cadaver-gun was trained on him, not Geller. She had a dark look, a troubled expression that, Pikul sensed, meant she was planning something. She said now, "You're with the Realist underground. Nader was not."

"Right." Carlaw seemed pleased she was starting to unravel the connections between the three men. He kept the gun leveled at Pikul, but now he was addressing her. "I was planted here to keep an eye on Nader. We suspected he was no longer to be trusted."

"You don't have to threaten us, Hugo Carlaw," Geller said.

He stared at her calmly. He toyed with the gun's clawlike hammer, then at last returned the weapon to its place on the shelf behind him.

"So if Nourish wasn't our real contact," Pikul said, relieved now that the gun wasn't pointing at him, "who is he?"

"Nourish is a double agent for Cortical Systematics. He was working with Nader ostensibly to aid him, but in fact to subvert the Realist cause. He was doing it rather well." Carlaw made a snorting sound, directing it at Pikul. "After all, he got you to assassinate the very man you were supposed to contact."

"It was a game urge," Pikul repeated.

"So you say. Well, you can at least do something to put matters right. You're going to have to put a stop to him."

"We are?" Pikul said.

"I assume you're both fitted with spinal-port inserts? With what you call bioports?"

"We are."

"Are they industry standard?"

"Well," Pikul said, "I've been wondering about that—"

"Yes," Geller said quickly, interrupting him. "Yes, they are standard."

A sudden fanatical zeal shone in Carlaw's eyes, and he briefly raised a clenched fist and waved it in the general direction of the sky.

"Don't you realize what that means?" he cried.

"Um . . . it means we can port into games?" Geller said.

"It means that neither of you can be buried on hallowed ground! Because you carry these . . . these *mutilations!* Did your bioport manual warn you of that little known detail?"

"I never read hardware manuals," Pikul said. "I just plug and play."

"Are you trying to talk us into having the bioports removed?" Geller said to him in a quiet, serious tone.

"No, no. The heresy has been committed and for you there is no going back! No forgiveness, no hallowed ground. Besides, you would be useless to us without your bioports. We Realists are of course forbidden to use them, and so on occasion we have to depend on people like you."

"I don't understand what you're saying, Carlaw." Geller had a feisty look on her face. She'd been looking troublesome ever since they discovered Nader's body. "Are you saying you want us to jack a game into our bioports?"

"A game?" Carlaw replied, with a creepy smile. "No, not a game. A weapon. This is in deadly earnest. No one is playing at this. You are to go back to the Trout Farm right away. In a familiar place you will find a moldy old wicker basket with a threadbare canvas cover."

"How will we know what to do?" Pikul asked.

"Even a child would know what to do," Carlaw replied, and his smile widened.

Behind him, someone knocked on the closed door of the stockroom, but Carlaw appeared to pay no attention. As the rapping intensified, Pikul gestured toward the door with his thumb.

"Aren't you going to get that?" he asked.

But Carlaw was now rocking quietly back and

forth on his heels, and Geller had vanished from beside him. Briefly, Pikul thought he was alone. Then the stockroom, with the ghastly remains of Nader's body, the racks of game-pods, the sickly smell of sudden death, all were fading away.

[21]

The walls dissolved, then solidified again. In the midst of the transition from one reality to another, Pikul felt his senses reeling out, urging to find a base of solidity or at least familiarity. He stared at a point on one wall, a place where a bare, overhead section of wood ran into the unpainted surface of a sloping roof. He identified it quickly: an A-frame, unvarnished natural timber beams, a wooden chalet, high mountains above the snow line, ski club.

Next to him, Geller had reappeared, sprawling with him on the bed with the UmbyCord snaking between them.

There was an unused bed against the next wall, the top coverlet unturned. Pikul had barely noticed it when they first came into this room.

It was now occupied.

D'Arcy Nader's body lay there in a terrible, contorted shape, his legs twisted unnaturally beneath his body. His head was thrown back at a horrible angle.

The knocking continued insistently. It was coming from the main door to the cabin.

Still confused, Pikul said, "Yeah . . . ?"

"Sorry to interrupt. Can you hear me?"

It was Kiri Vinokur's voice, outside the chalet door.

"We're here, Kiri!" Geller called, glancing at Pikul as if to reassure herself he was all right.

Pikul hissed urgently, "Allegra . . . Nader's on the other bed!"

She turned her head in shock, saw the grotesque corpse lying there. Her eyes widened in terror and disgust. The door handle was turning.

Geller yelled at the door, "Don't come in, Kiri! Give us just one moment!"

They both saw through the frosted window that Vinokur's shadow moved back from the door.

"How the hell did Nader get there?" Pikul demanded of her.

"I don't know! It doesn't make sense!" She crawled against him, the UmbyCord stretching behind her. She looked in horror at Nader's body. "He was a game character! Not a real person!"

"You take the words out of my mouth. What in hell is he doing here, in this room?"

"Let me think, let me think!"

She stared at Nader with a desperate expression

on her face. Outside, the shadow moved again.

"Allegra, ist there any problem?"

"Just getting my clothes on!" Geller called, with a semblance of a guilty laugh. Then she clutched Pikul's wrist. "Look, Nader's starting to fade away. I can explain it!"

"Go on, then."

"It's what we call game residue. When you have a particularly vivid image in a game, something horrific, frightening, even something supremely beautiful, then an image of it can persist for a short while into reality. It's a common phenomenon in some games, but I didn't know it could happen in *eXistenZ*. I'll have to remember to look into that, next time I'm coding."

"I think I should be coming in now!" Vinokur said from outside the door.

"That's okay, Kiri," Pikul called. "We're both decent."

The door opened at once and Vinokur stepped in. He was holding a large wooden tray laden with dishes.

"I thought you'd better be having something to eat," he said. "We've knocked on the door a few times to invite you for dinner, but we couldn't get an answer—"

"We've been kind of tied up," Pikul said, indicating the UmbyCord.

"When I am getting no answer, I figured you were playing *eXistenZ*, trying out the new pod and the bioport. Everything ist working all right, I take it? As you expect it to be?"

Geller was blushing, Pikul suddenly noticed. At the same time he realized how awkward he too felt. Vinokur's arrival gave him the same unmistakable feeling he'd often had as a teenager, when an early returning parent sometimes surprised him in a darkened front room with his girlfriend. There was undoubtedly something deeply intimate about porting in with another person, especially one so young and attractive as Allegra Geller.

Vinokur had obviously picked up on the feeling as well. As he came into the room and kicked the door closed behind him with a heel, then crossed to the table, he kept his gaze averted.

"Shall I just be leaving the tray here for you?" he asked.

"Yeah," Pikul said. "Thanks. On the table will do."

"Don't bother with the unporting," Vinokur said. "I am only wanting to be sure our star designer ist in good shape, and safe, and rested . . . and that she has recovered her multimillion dollar game system from her repaired pod."

The tray rattled as he put it down on the table. They noticed that all the dishes were covered with inverted plates, to keep the food warm.

"Thanks so much, Kiri," Geller said. "This is very sweet of you."

Vinokur straightened. "So I take it she is," he said after an awkward pause.

"I am what?" Geller asked.

"Is recovered. The lost *eXistenZ* is recovered."

"Oh, yeah. Sure. That's why you find us like this. Spaced out, not sure of reality." Geller grinned and shrugged her shoulders in a play of dippy enthusiasm. "Wow. You know."

"Wow," Pikul said supportively.

"We were right into it, weren't we?" Geller said to him.

"We were. And it's amazing."

"That's a relief," Vinokur said. "Well, I'll be leaving you two young people alone again. You can be leaving the tray outside your door when you have finished."

"As a matter of interest," Pikul said. "What is it you've brought us?"

"Believe it or not, it ist Chinese food. There ist a most wonderful restaurant on the other side of the escarpment road."

He turned to go.

"Kiri?" Geller said.

"Yes?"

"Have you heard any news yet? I mean, about the *eXistenZ* test seminar and the shooting that happened there?"

"Oh yes. It was showing on all the TV channels. You've never been more famous. Your face ist everywhere, which of course just makes it worse. I . . ."

His voice trailed away.

"What?" Geller said. "Tell me."

"It ist having an unwanted effect. You know how audience-conscious the whole game world is. Companies like Antenna are positioning themselves in the marketplace. Ist the need to maximize their capital investment. The decision ist nothing to do with me, let me say now."

"What decision is nothing to do with you, Kiri?" Geller said in a thin voice.

"All right. Don't be shooting the messenger, ist the only thing I ask. They have announced the possibility that Antenna will indefinitely be delaying the release of your new system. They are wanting to do some market research, quantify some demographics . . . that ist how they are putting it. They want to determine how widespread the support for this fanatical group really is. Me, I'm out of such things. I don't approve. We shouldn't bend one degree to extremism, ist where I stand. You know that that's always been my position. Anyway, a game is a game. That ist all it ist."

Geller took this in, biting her lower lip. "Shit!" she said. "The rats are betraying me."

"I knew you would not be being too happy when you found out."

"Happy isn't the word," Pikul said.

"Support for the fanatics?" Geller said. "What does that mean?"

"Well, you know. They're all coming out of the woodwork now."

"Who are?"

Vinokur looked away unhappily, and sighed.

"There ist a certain number of people who are taking the opportunity to leap on the antigame bandwagon. You know who they are; they're always around in the background somewhere. They are being a fact of life for game companies. They are hearing these rumors about what some other people say *eXistenZ* ist, and they don't go any further. They don't worry about facts. Why should they, when their minds are made up? So, they say we haff gone too far this time. Psychologically, medically, socially . . . you name it. Antenna has image-control consultants working full-time on fielding the kind of wild balls they throw at us. So they aren't a major worry.

"The trouble ist, the real trouble ist, that this plays into the hands of our business competitors. The bottom line ist of course that Antenna ist a corporation to be making money. It's a business, and money always ist counting. This kind of adverse publicity ist heaven-sent to competitors. They can't beat *eXistenZ* on the ground; we all know that. It's the finest game system in the world. And because of you they can't even be replicating game shells that look like *eXistenZ*. So they can't beat it, but they think whipping up the hysteria against it might be a way of killing it anyway. Or at least putting it back."

"Yeah, yeah. I'm beginning to see that."

Geller was still looking thoughtfully at the tray of untouched food.

"What can I do?" she said, almost to herself.

"Why don't we be repositioning you with Antenna again?" Vinokur said. "Are you sure you don't want me to be contacting the company? Even just to be finding out what they have to say?"

"No, Kiri. Not yet."

He shrugged, and she gave him a quick, affectionate hug.

"Well, enjoy your meal," he said. "That's what waiters say, isn't it?"

"Okay, Kiri," Geller said. "We'll talk with you later." He was halfway through the door. "And thanks for everything," she added.

He waved a hand back to them as he closed the door.

Pikul waited until Vinokur's footsteps faded away down the sloping path outside, then gestured toward the door.

"Your friend Kiri is getting shaky," he said. "My guess is he's about to turn you in to Antenna."

"That sounds like you might approve."

Her expression was hard and challenging, and Pikul mentally recoiled from her.

"I keep thinking about the choices," he said. "You know, staying in hiding until everything calms down. That sort of thing. It can't be long before somebody at Antenna thinks of looking for you here, for instance. Maybe approaching the company now, on your own terms, might be the safest thing." He noticed that Geller was staring at the tray of food Vinokur had brought. "Are you hungry?"

She grinned at him. "Are you kidding?" she said.

"Me neither. For one thing, I'm terrified of even looking under the plates. How does the thought of sweet and sour tadpole grab you?"

He picked up the tray and moved it to the other side of the chalet room.

"Pikul, what do you think of what Kiri was saying, about there being support for these fanatics?"

"It doesn't sound good to me. Maybe we should after all stop—"

"We can't stop," Geller said. "While we've been playing, I've noticed some new things about *eXistenZ* . . . glitches. D'Arcy Nader coming through as game residue has made me think. These things need looking at, and maybe debugging. I don't know what they could mean to the whole system. They mean to me that I'm not sure the game is okay anymore."

Pikul sat down next to her and looked as sympathetic as he knew how.

"Listen," he said. "Do you want to know what I think, what I really think?"

"Sure."

"You might not like it."

"I'll take that chance," Geller said.

He took a deep breath. Then he said, "Okay, to be honest, I find your game confusing. I'm not convinced I want to go back in there, because I don't completely believe I'm going to keep coming out again. You know, the sense we might be trapped there. Or that when we do come out, it's not going to be to the same place we left."

"That's part of the game experience," Geller said coolly.

"Do you really like that feeling?"

"I *love* it!" she replied. "Look, when *eXistenZ* is finally released it's going to wipe the competition off the face of the earth."

He sighed to himself, realizing that what he'd said was not getting through to her.

"Will it?" he asked.

"You bet! It really will be the supreme game, the one that all the others are judged against." She shifted position, looking thoughtful. After a while she looked him straight in the eye and said, "Don't hurt me, Pikul. Not now, after all this. Don't make me go back in there alone. Keep playing with me."

"Allegra, I'm worried that the game is going to

wipe *me* off the face of the earth. I'm beginning to think I was right all along not to have a bioport installed."

She moved quickly, turning around to face him. "But it's too late for that. And you're ported in."

She mischievously flicked the Play nipple on the pod, and before Pikul could react, the walls of the chalet began to melt away around them.

[22]

There was smoke swirling ahead, brilliantly illuminated from behind by white arc lamps. Two men were silhouetted against the billowing luminescence, working endlessly with raised batons or sticks, prodding, feeling, stroking with them. A long line of people shuffled slowly in the direction of the guards, their faces turned indifferently toward the ground, their shoulders stooped.

Everyone was hemmed in by the walls of a long corridor, which firmed up around Pikul and Geller as reality took hold.

A large-built woman with a puffy face was walking slowly down the line of people, holding a clipboard. Several sheets of paper were held in place on this, curling and lifting in the draft while she moved along. As she passed each person she peered intently at their ID cards, checking their faces against the photographs and names on the clipboard.

She reached Geller and Pikul, conducting the same check. Her eyes were dull with boredom, her face rigid with fatigue. She muttered their names: Barb Brecken and Larry Ashen.

Recovering from the sudden transition of realities, Pikul glanced down at his own badge to check the identity, then looked across at Geller beside him.

"That was cruel," he said to her. "You knew I didn't want to be here again."

"It wasn't cruel, it was desperate. We've come this far, we've got to see the game through to the end. C'mon, Pikul . . . this is a typical case of first-time user anxiety, and you've got it bad."

"Yeah, all right," he conceded. "But I don't like it here. I don't know what's going on. We're just blundering around in the dark. This world is unformed, and we don't know the limits. We only know some of the moves: assembly of bioelectronic parts, the manufacture of undetectable weapons, a Chinese restaurant in the woods, an old trout farm full of mutated frogs. You've never explained what the game objectives are, or how we hope to achieve them. All the clues are indecipherable, at least to me. Maybe they don't even exist. And on top of all that, there are people out there who are actively trying to kill us."

They stepped forward together as the line moved on. Geller suddenly squeezed his hand.

"That sounds like my game," she said. "You're catching on at last."

They were now within a few paces of the security area at the end of the corridor, and could see that the two guards were frisking everyone who entered. They were using electronic wands almost identical to the one Pikul had been issued at the church hall meeting.

"You mean all this is deliberate?" Pikul said.

"It's programmed that way, yes."

"You designed the Chinese restaurant?" he said incredulously.

"No, I designed the parameters within which the Chinese restaurant might be created from the players' subconscious. We made it all. We're still making it all."

"This corridor?"

"Okay . . . anyone can do corridors," she said. "Game designers have clip libraries of images they can draw on."

"Yeah, I know all that. Or I'm learning about it. It still sounds like a game that's not going to be easy to market."

"But it's a game that everyone already plays. We call it *eXistenZ*, everyone else knows it as Existence. It's life, Pikul. It's reality. It doesn't have to be marketed. We simply let the world know it's ready, and the world moves in and joins *eXistenZ*.

It's a self-marketing product. It's wonderful!"

"So you say."

They each submitted to the electronic test. Pikul was on his guard because he wasn't sure what the security guards were looking for and if he might inadvertently be carrying it. In fact, he was cleared quickly.

Geller was taking longer. She stood upright before the security guard. Pikul noticed the way the man moved his wand rather too slowly and lasciviously across her body. He scanned her breasts and backside thoroughly. Geller didn't seem to mind too much. Pikul was about to step forward, get the man off her, when she too was cleared and she stepped across to him.

"Something bothering you?" she said.

"No, Allegra. You wrote everything in this game, right?"

"What's eating you now?"

"A question I'm always asking myself in this place." He bit back his feelings because he was learning at last that there were answers or explanations for everything he didn't like, and he didn't always like the answers either.

They passed through the security zone and emerged into the long assembly hut. They were not alone: it was the time a new shift was due to begin, and the other workers they'd lined up with were drifting around the enclosed space, moving in a desultory fashion toward their various assembly cubicles. Meanwhile, the workers finishing their shifts were easing off, stretching their arms, turning over the assembly bays to their replacements.

Meanwhile, the conveyor belt continued to move with its sinister load between the bays.

"Remind me," Pikul said. "What exactly are we looking for here?"

"What Hugo Carlaw told us about. A moldy old wicker basket with a threadbare canvas cover. And it will be found in what he described as a familiar place."

"Can you think of anywhere in this building that you or I would consider familiar?"

"Your assembly cubicle? Mine?"

"We can skip the one I was using," Pikul said. "No room for anything apart from the operator and a small box. Let's start with yours."

They walked through to the back of the components building and went down the shallow ramp leading to the pod assembly area where Barb Brecken worked. The familiar smell of horse dung drifted into their nostrils. Geller led the way to the last bay, and they slipped inside.

For the moment, no one was there. Several game-pods, in various stages of assembly, lay on the surgically equipped worktables.

Pikul spotted the wicker basket almost immediately. It had been left casually in the farthest corner of the bay, covered by an unmistakably threadbare canvas sheet. There appeared to be something lumpy inside.

He strode over to it and Geller followed.

She knelt down and began to unwrap the sheet from the contents. Pikul stood guard.

"I'd say it's exactly as advertised," Geller said, looking down as she lifted the covers away.

In the basket was a game-pod, and when Geller stripped away the final wrap, Pikul could see the whole thing.

It was not in good shape, to say the least. Something biological or organic had eaten away at it, eroding and discoloring the outer shell, infecting the innards. The pod had dark, necrotic patches of hard scar tissue, and where a normal game-pod would be stippled with red, this one had garish streaks of purple.

"God, it's ugly!" Pikul said. "Even for a game-pod."

Geller was still staring down at it with a fixed expression.

"Come on," Pikul said. "Let's go. We found what we came to find."

"No, wait."

Something was exciting Geller; he could hear it in her voice.

"I have a terrible urge to port into that pod," she said. "What about you?"

"Oh, sure," he replied, disbelieving what he'd

heard. "Yes, you could say I'm desperate to port into that diseased, gangrenous, moldering, dying heap of organism. Let me at it! I can hardly wait."

"Sarcasm doesn't become you," Geller said.

She straightened and went across to a large pile of UmbyCords draped over a peg. She pulled one of the Cords off at random and quickly checked to see if it was complete and functional. She sat down on a rotten wooden folding chair next to the death-pod's basket and with a great deal of care ported in one end of the UmbyCord.

"Okay," she said, "here we go. Will you give me a hand at the back there? I can't reach around it on my own."

"You're not serious, Geller! I mean, this is a significantly diseased pod! Once you port into it, God alone knows what you'll become. You'll—"

"Exactly," she said. "The game unfolds, the next level awaits. Help me with the UmbyCord."

She pulled up her shirt to reveal her bioport, and with deep reluctance Pikul knelt down beside her. He took the active end of the UmbyCord and slipped it into the port at the base of her spine.

"You satisfied with that?" he asked. "Everything feels good?"

"Yes."

"How long will it take for the pod infection to take hold of you?"

"No time at all," Geller said. Something about her voice sounded unusual, and Pikul glanced quickly up at her.

"And then you quietly port into all the other pods and spread the infection to them . . . "

"Oh, *God*!" Geller went rigid.

"What's happening?"

"Something's wrong. Seriously wrong! Unport me, Pikul, quickly!"

"Okay, I'll get to it."

He lifted away the thin covering fabric of her shirt with a snatching motion, but in the few seconds since he'd ported her into the pod, the bioport had swollen up grotesquely. It now seemed to be bulging up and around, like a fist gripping the jack plug. It had turned an alarming scarlet color and bulged perilously at its extremities. He pulled at it, but nothing shifted.

He pulled again, this time tugging it harder.

"Don't do that!" Geller shouted, doubling up. "Oh God, that *really* hurts!"

"Sorry. It seems to be caught."

"That's obviously not the way. Try something else! Hurry, though! I can feel it starting to get to me!"

Pikul let go of the UmbyCord and looked around for something else to try with.

The death-pod, apparently triggered by Pikul's attempt to disconnect it from Geller, was starting to convulse in a series of violent peristaltic spasms. Each disgusting ripple produced a consequent response in Geller, who looked as if she was being wrestled to death by the movements. Pikul searched desperately for something to use against the pod.

He spotted a clutch of tools hanging from a long metal rack on the wall. One of the tools was a sharp-bladed linoleum knife.

"I'll cut you free!" he shouted. "It's the only way."

"No!" Geller cried. "Not a cut! I've always been afraid of knives."

"I won't hurt you."

With a sense of terrible loathing he slashed violently at the quivering UmbyCord. A lateral gash immediately appeared, with blood fountaining up in a fine spray from the slit. Horrified by what he'd done, and more by the fact that the UmbyCord had not been severed, Pikul slashed again. Then a third time.

The UmbyCord snapped in half at last, and shrank back as if until that moment it had been stretched. Blood was gushing from both ends where he'd made the cut.

"What have you done?" Geller cried in panic. "Pikul, if that doesn't stop, I'm going to bleed to death!"

He looked around frantically, desperate to find something with which to stanch the flow, but in the poorly lit and squalid stable there was nothing suitable. In desperation he stamped his foot down on Geller's end of the cord. The main flow of blood stopped immediately, although some continued to leak out slowly around his foot.

Geller moaned in despair and misery.

"I'm sorry, Geller," Pikul said. "I didn't know what else to do!"

A man's voice said, "I do."

Pikul whirled around, managing to maintain his foot's pressure on the end of the cord. It was Yevgeny Nourish who had spoken. He'd entered the stall while they were preoccupied.

"I know exactly what to do," Nourish said with horrible menace.

Nourish was in the process of taking a large propane torch from a hook on the wall. He slipped the straps over his shoulder and unscrewed the gas valve. A fierce hissing immediately followed.

"For God's sake!" Geller cried, her eyes frantic. "What are you doing?"

Nourish ignited the torch, and a long blue-white flame stabbed out, roaring a deadly heat into the confined space of the stall.

"Death to Realism!" Nourish shouted.

He turned the cone of flame on the death-pod in the basket, standing over it with an expression of appalling relish on his face. The pod reacted at once to the blast of heat: it shriveled and crackled, and bubbles of what looked like boiling fat erupted on its diseased surface. A smell of burning flesh, human or animal, pervaded the stall, a disgusting stench of decay and death.

The pod was trying to save itself, rippling away from the deadly flame like a trapped centipede. Wherever the flame played, the pod's dying body hunched away defensively.

Nourish laughed maniacally, and began to play the flame over the entire surface of the pod, deliberately picking out those parts that were arching away from him.

Geller sank to the ground in a state of apparent shock, holding on to Pikul's leg for support.

Now the stricken pod was starting to swell under the terrible jetting inferno. Immense bubbles kept erupting up to its surface, to burst with gaseous explosions as the flame hit them. Inside the pod, more frightening changes could be seen taking place: a broiling dark gas was swirling about angrily under the transparent integument of the pod, flecked with bright red points. The entire pod was swelling, growing, starting to bulge . . .

It exploded without warning, scattering charred pieces of burned flesh in all directions.

A bulging, bellowing cloud of gas burst forth, a solid jet of dark smoke, black and gray, oily and viscous, and belching out of the shattered, melted remains of the pod with a force that seemed impossible for the size of the thing.

Nourish staggered backward in reaction to the volcano of black smoke, the propane flame flashing dangerously around the small space like the glittering blade of a razor-sharp sword. Pikul ducked away as the flame arced by him, and Geller clung more tightly to his leg.

The black smoke appeared to have a life of its own. Instead of filling and choking the air of the stall, it shot upward in a steady jet then spread sideways along the roof above the adjacent stalls, heading toward the main area of the Trout Farm's assembly line.

As it spread out it cooled. A gritty ash, rather like tiny grains of coal, began to settle on all the areas below.

Nourish clearly had had no idea this was going to happen, because he watched the progress of the vile cloud with a horrified expression. The propane jet flared down, threateningly close to the dung-stiff straw that lay everywhere on the floor of the stall.

Gathering up her last shreds of energy, Geller rose to a kneeling position. She drew back from Pikul. He turned to help her but to his amazement saw that she was about to pounce on him. She dived hard, shouldering him aside so that his foot came away from the end of the sliced-apart UmbyCord. Blood pulsed anew from the open end.

As Pikul staggered away, off balance, Geller grabbed the linoleum knife from his inert hand.

Trailing her bloody cord, she lunged at Nourish, driving the blood-smeared blade deep into his back, twisting it, hacking downward for maximum effect.

Nourish screamed with pain, drooped forward, managed to recover his poise, then turned in her direction. She stood in shock, paralyzed by his response.

He raised the propane torch toward her face and staggered menacingly forward. The flame waved from side to side in a deadly arc.

"*Death!*" he croaked. "Death to the demoness . . . death to Barb Brecken . . . death to the game—"

Pikul said, stupidly, "Death to who?" He saw Geller's ID card swinging between her breasts. "Oh yeah . . . Barb . . . "

Nourish's eyeballs rolled upward in a final dying spasm, and he croaked his last. He slumped forward into the brown-smeared straw, the propane torch jetting its flame into the tinder-dry material.

A ball of flame exploded up around him, mixing with the jet of black smoke that continued to belch out of the pod.

Pikul leaped through the sheet of flame that had erupted between him and Geller. Her cord was still trailing, still pulsing blood everywhere. In desperation, he grabbed it. He twisted it fiercely in his hands, strangling it. After a few more spurts, the blood was finally stanched.

In the few seconds that this took, the fire had spread throughout most of the stall. The straw was now ablaze in many places, and the flames were already shooting up the wooden walls. The doorway was a rectangle of white liquid fire, roaring fiercely with backdraft as the air from outside rushed into the vacuum in the stall created by the inferno.

Both he and Geller were starting to choke, and tears were streaming from their eyes.

Outside, above the terrible sounds of the conflagration, they could hear the rest of the assembly plant reacting to the emergency. Several sirens started howling together. A voice on the loudspeaker system began uttering a series of evacuation orders. A bell was ringing insistently and deafeningly. People were screaming and shouting and Pikul could hear a huge crowd of them running unseen down the passage outside the stalls. Such fear was infectious: Pikul felt a pandemonium of panic in his mind, a quest to run, escape, hide.

Meanwhile, the flames were racing across the straw on which they stood, licking up at them. The smoke made it almost impossible to breathe.

Pikul held Geller tightly in his arms. She was limp, drained, at the end of everything. He wondered if she were still even capable of knowing he was there with her.

As the flames engulfed them, Pikul said softly, "I think we just lost the game, Geller."

But as terminal darkness spread around them, strange and inexplicable shapes could be glimpsed through the flames: a chair, a bed, a bathtub, a table.

The guest chalet was morphing into form around them.

"Or maybe not," Pikul said softly to her.

[**23**]

They were together on the bed in the chalet. Allegra Geller was in his arms. The room was gently lit by low-power lamps, and the quiet darkness of the valley night was soft against the windows. As reality swam into being, Pikul cherished these few moments of peace. The deadly inferno of the Trout Farm was behind them, the unknown lay ahead, but at least for the moment he had Allegra Geller safe in his arms and they were alone on a bed.

As the shape of the guest chalet morphed up around them, he began to feel increasingly concerned about Allegra's well-being. Although she was breathing steadily and seemed at peace, she showed no signs of emerging from the physical and mental collapse that had followed the violence in the pod-assembly stall. Maybe she was suffering aftereffects, or a kind of shock . . .

Even so, he loved the feel of her body in his arms. He bent his face tenderly toward hers.

She stirred at last, so he laid his fingers on her cheek.

"Allegra?"

She groaned lightly.

"Allegra, we're back home. At the ski club. Can you hear me?"

"Yeah," she said indistinctly.

"Is anything wrong?"

"I always get a kick out of returning from a game. Sometimes I experience a little extra and then I like to take my time. The extra now is that you're here with me. I like you holding me."

She opened her eyes and looked dreamily up at him, but almost immediately a harsh comprehension entered her eyes.

"Pikul, it's here with us!" she said with obvious alarm. She sat up and swiveled around to face him directly. "It's happened," she said. "It came back with us. We must have brought it back with us when we came out of *eXistenZ.*"

"We brought what back?" Pikul said obtusely. "I don't understand what you're saying."

"We brought the disease back with us! My game-pod is infected."

She was now fully alert.

As if realizing for the first time the implications of what she was saying, Allegra leaped up from the bed and stood before him. She reached behind her, trying

234

to pull at the UmbyCord, still connected not only to the game-pod on the bed but also to her spine.

"My God, I'm really going to lose it this time! I'm going to lose my game! Unport me, Pikul! Come on, get the damned thing out of me!"

Pikul swiftly unported her—now that they were back in reality, there were no problems in removing the Cord from the bioport—and she danced away from him in evident relief. She turned and bent over the game-pod, which remained on the bed, close to where they'd been lying together so intimately.

Pikul reached behind him and tried to get the UmbyCord out of his own bioport, but it was held stiffly in place. He walked crabwise the short distance across to a wall mirror and contorted himself to see better. Although the Cord was still tightly implanted in him, there did not appear to be any abnormal swelling or discoloration around the bioport.

Just the completely normal swelling and discoloration, he thought.

Geller had moved to her shoulder bag. She searched around inside it and after a moment pulled out a tiny hypodermic needle sealed inside a sterile pack.

She unwrapped the needle quickly, plucked off the polythene stopper that protected the point, then held the syringe up to the light and flicked any bubbles out of the liquid. She squirted a microspray into the air.

Kneeling beside the bed, she put her free hand on the game-pod.

"I'm here," she said softly to the game-pod, as if it were a sick child. "I'm here with you."

She thrust the needle into the side of the pod. As she pushed in the plunger she massaged the rest of the pod with her free hand, using a series of sensual strokes that looked to Pikul as if she was starting to make love to it. He almost expected her to press her open lips to it and give it mouth-to-mouth resuscitation.

While he continued to struggle with his own end of the UmbyCord, careful not to pull at it so hard that he dislodged the game-pod from the bed, Pikul realized the full significance of what Geller had said.

"Did you say we've brought the disease back?" he asked. "I mean . . . in one sense it doesn't surprise me, because that was such a horrible experience. But surely that would be impossible? We were in a game. It wasn't reality. How can a game event have any effect on real life?"

Geller glanced back at him while she continued to massage the pod.

"There's obviously some kind of weird reality bleed-through going on here," she said. "I'm not sure I get it."

Pikul's bioport suddenly released the jack of the UmbyCord, which came out with an audible popping sound.

"What's in that syringe you're using?" Pikul asked.

"It's a broad-spectrum sporicide. I'm not sure what the hell it was I picked up in the assembly bay, but all game-pods are congenitally susceptible to spores, pollen, and airborne fungi. Clinically, the RNA of spore infection is usually one of a range of known sequences, and so what I've jabbed in will probably help. The main thing is to get to it in time."

While she was speaking, Pikul had been scratching unconsciously at his bioport. Geller noticed this and fixed him with an intense look.

"You got an itch?" she said.

"Sorry. Am I irritating you?"

"No. Let me see your bioport."

"What?"

"Let me see it, Pikul!"

Reluctantly, Pikul turned his back toward her. She examined it so closely he could feel the light, passing pressure of her breath on his skin.

"I think I've figured out what must have happened," she said in a low and dismal voice. "It must have been Kiri Vinokur. I can't believe he would do such a thing. That bastard."

Pikul could sense the anger in her.

"I thought Vinokur was your friend," he said, once again feeling the unpleasant rising of paranoia.

"I can't be sure of anything anymore. He installed this bioport, didn't he?"

"Yes. I mean, oh no!"

"What?"

"I think I see what you're driving at."

"He must have deliberately given you another infected bioport, so that when we jacked in together, my pod would become infected and ultimately die. As would my game system."

"I'm infected?" Pikul said in sudden panic. "Wait a minute!"

"There was no reality bleed-through after all," Geller said. "We were thinking about it from the wrong direction. When we were in the game, the poor thing was trying to tell us that it was sick. It was the pod that introduced the theme of disease into the game."

"The *theme* of disease?"

"It wasn't real."

"It might not have been real in the game, but back here in the real world I'm fucking infected! Is it going to crawl up my spine and rot my brain?"

She stared at him impatiently for a moment, but then her expression changed. In a businesslike way she went back to her bag.

"All right, don't panic," she said. "I've got something that will help you."

She brusquely wiped away the tears that had filled her eyes while she attended to the pod, and took out a cork-shaped plastic capsule from her bag. She snapped it open to reveal a knurled, pluglike electronic device.

"This'll fix it."

"What is it?" Pikul asked.

"I'm going to seal up your bioport with a sporici-dal resonator." She bent over him and began easing the tiny instrument into his bioport. "It uses the Umby-Cord pickups for power. It should cleanse all your porting channels of infection in a few hours."

"Is it going to hurt?"

"Is it hurting now?" she said.

"No."

"Then it probably won't hurt later. It'll give you a little skin buzz when it's done. Of course, we can't go back into the game until then."

"Ouch! It's hurting now."

"Sorry. That was me."

When her hands moved away from him, Pikul pulled down his shirt and turned to face her once more.

"Look, this isn't over, is it?" he said. "We seem to be out of the game for the moment but that's surely not the end of it. What has happened here could be critical, if it's true. Are you really saying that you think Vinokur is an agent of the Anti-eXistenZialists?"

"It's beginning to look that way. It frightens me, but what other explanation could there be?"

"I don't know. All I'm sure of is that if he's one of them, then we really are in the—"

He stopped, because Geller had turned abruptly away from him.

"The pod!" she cried. "Something's happening! Pikul, it's dying!"

Sure enough, the pod had started quivering and rippling, turning a livid purple color in streaks. Geller fell to her knees against the side of the bed, reaching out to cradle it.

"I can't give it any help," she said dismally. "There's nothing I can do for it."

Her head drooped down toward it.

At that moment, without warning, there was a brilliant white-orange flash from outside and their windows and door blew in explosively. Shattered glass and wood flew about their heads.

[24]

Geller had been shielded from the worst effects of the blast by the bed, but Pikul was thrown off his feet. He tumbled and rolled across the polished pine floorboards while debris crashed all around him.

The pressure wave passed as quickly as it had come, and after a few seconds of confusion Pikul recovered, impelled by his fear of what the blast might have done to Geller. He climbed incautiously to his feet, the rubble cascading off him. He felt around his body, checking the vital organs. He was bruised and scratched in many places, but as far as he could tell, he'd suffered no serious harm.

He clambered in a state of intense anxiety across the rubble-strewn floor.

The hot glare still shone beyond the now glassless window frame, and waves of heat were billowing into the room.

It was eerily silent, but for the roar of the fire outside their chalet.

He reached Geller, and although she was severely shocked and shaken by the tremendous explosion, she appeared unhurt.

"What the hell was that about?" Pikul asked.

She glanced around the shattered room with a deeply fearful expression. Her face was white and her hands were shaking.

"I'm frightened," she said miserably. "Pikul, I'm so dreadfully frightened . . . "

They peeked wide-eyed together through the window.

The chalet next to theirs had been destroyed by the massive explosion and was now completely engulfed in flames. Even as they watched, the one remaining upright wall collapsed backward into the inferno, sending sparks flying a hundred feet into the night air. Another wave of heat battered at them. The whole valley seemed to be infused by the orange glare.

"Listen!" Geller said. "People are coming."

A pandemonium of shouting voices and roaring engines could be heard from lower down the mountain, as the other occupants of the ski club reacted to the catastrophe and started to rush up to this area by any means they could. Already there were men moving around the scene of the inferno outside their chalet, grappling with emergency fire hoses and unrolling them.

Pikul and Geller moved away cautiously from their temporary shelter behind the bed.

A figure suddenly appeared silhouetted in the doorway, the light of the fires flickering over his face.

It was Hugo Carlaw. He was cradling a submachine gun in his arms.

As soon as he saw Pikul and Geller, he began to scream at them.

"The uprising has begun!" he bellowed. "The whole place is on fire! Let's go! You've got to get out of here! They'll be looking for you."

Pikul said to Geller, "Carlaw the cashier? He's a game character! How the hell can he be here?"

"I don't know! I don't know!"

Carlaw strode into the room, grabbed Geller by the back of her shirt and jerked her to her feet. She tried to grab her game-pod, but Carlaw kicked it away from her. It skidded across the floor.

"Leave that piece of rotting meat here!" he said harshly. "It's done its job. Let it die."

"But my game!" Geller cried. "My game's inside. I don't want my game to die!"

His face rigid with loathing, Carlaw unslung his machine gun and cocked it. He took casual aim at the game-pod, then released a ferocious hail of bullets at it. In a fraction of a second her irreplaceable, almost priceless game-pod had been blown into messy streaks of flesh and organism that spread in an unrecoverable slime over the rubble from the explosion.

Geller whimpered, and seemed to shrink back into herself. With her shoulders huddled, she could only stare silently at the end of her dreams.

Pikul took her hand. "Geller?" he said. She did not respond, so Pikul reached over and swiveled her around so she was facing him. "Allegra!"

She was in shock.

Pikul brought his face just inches from hers. "Allegra, listen to me!" he said loudly, trying to shut out everything around them, including the threatening presence of Carlaw only a short distance behind him. "It's not as bad as it seems! I think we're still *inside* the game. We haven't moved back to reality, but we must be inside a subset of the game that is supposed to look and feel like reality. No other explanation makes sense. Think about it! First the diseased pod is here with us, now Carlaw is. We know for sure that both are only creations of the game. They come from your subconscious or mine."

He paused to draw breath, and cast a glance at Carlaw. In silent confirmation of Pikul's theory, the man now appeared to be rocking gently back and forth. The confusion outside was too noisy to allow Pikul to hear if he was humming.

"If that's so," Pikul went on, as the idea took hold,

"then your real pod must still be out there somewhere. Somewhere safe. I think we can let this one go, this game-pod. It's not the real one anymore."

She nodded. She was still in shock, but had somehow managed to take that in.

There was more shouting outside, this time much closer than before. Then, to their horror, a Molotov cocktail came sailing into the room through the broken window and shattered against the end of the bed. It exploded instantly and the bed went up in a sheet of flame.

All three of them ducked defensively away as the deadly conflagration burst around them.

"Everybody out!" Carlaw shouted. "*Now*!"

They rushed outside, scrambling over the rubble and broken glass on the ground outside the chalet. The whole area was lit by the roaring inferno of the next chalet. The cool mountain air was full of the choking stench of burning; the night was alive with flying sparks.

As they stood there, taking in what was happening, there was another explosion. A chalet farther down the mountain track burst into flames.

"Hadn't we better help?" Pikul shouted, seeing the swarm of people dashing around, trying to do something about the fires. An appliance had materialized from somewhere, and more fire fighters in bright yellow helmets were unrolling their hoses and starting to play water on the flames.

"Help?" Carlaw cried sardonically. "No, you two are coming with me."

To encourage them, he cocked his semiautomatic gun again, and aimed it at them.

"Up the hill!" he ordered. "Now!"

Another explosion, another fireball, another chalet added to the terrible light in the valley.

Geller hesitated, looking back in anguish at the spreading destruction of the ski club.

"This is all my fault!" she wailed.

"Come on, Allegra," Pikul said. "Let's do what the man says."

Carlaw snapped back into action. "Up the hill!" he ordered again. "Now!"

A path led away from the sea of burning destruction, up narrowly through the shrubs and smaller trees, into the peacefulness of the ancient pinewoods above, where the ground was soft with centuries of mold and the air was no longer filled with acrid smoke.

As they climbed higher the sounds of the confusion faded, but still the clouded sky was reflecting a rich, glowing orange light down on them.

[25]

After a climb of several minutes, the path at last widened and flattened out, and they came to a small area of level but broken rocky ground, where no trees were growing.

Carlaw gestured back down toward the valley. "We can see everything from up here," he said.

"What exactly is it we're seeing?" Pikul said sardonically, looking at the destruction below. Two or three chalets were still burning fiercely, their smoke churning into the sky, but most of them were now merely smoldering. There was not one that was still intact.

"You're looking at the victory of Realism," Carlaw said. "And you two were a part of it."

Geller was holding Pikul's arm.

"It was the death of *eXistenZ*," she said. "We two were actually a part of that."

"Look down, young woman," Carlaw said. "See

what you have made, see what we have done with what you made. Enjoy it while you can."

His machine gun made a horrible and now all too familiar clicking noise. He raised it casually, pointing it at Geller.

"There's just one last thing before Reality is once more safe."

"What are you doing?" Pikul cried. "Surely we're on your side!"

"No way! How could you be? How could Allegra Geller, designer of the world's foremost game system, be on the side of Realism? All her work is profoundly anti-Realism."

"But my name is Barb Brecken," Geller said, as if on an inspiration.

"Cut it out, lady! We know who you are. You can't hide inside the false reality of a game forever."

"Something's slipped over the edge here," Pikul said, turning desperately toward Geller, knowing that this sort of action often had the effect of pausing the game. "Something's all wrong with this."

"You have to find a way to help me, Pikul," Geller said in a small, frightened voice.

"You see our problem, then," Carlaw said.

He raised the gun once more, and this time his intent was obvious and deliberate. All the previous casualness was gone from his movements. Illuminated harshly against the orange inferno below, he pointed the gun at Allegra's head and pulled the trigger.

But before the gun fired, he jolted to the side, his head turning violently at a wicked angle. He collapsed on the ground, the gun clattering onto the rocks around him. He lay sprawled at an uncomfortable angle between two jagged rocks, twitching.

Pikul and Geller froze with disbelief and terror.

Kiri Vinokur stepped out from the shelter of the closest trees and advanced warily toward the stricken man. He was holding what looked at first glance like a large dead rat, but that Pikul quickly identified as the cadaver-gun he himself had assembled in the Chinese restaurant.

Vinokur stepped carefully over the broken ground and went up to the moaning body of Carlaw.

Without hesitation, and with a steady hand, he fired the coup de grace into the back of Carlaw's head. The man jerked violently once more, then was still.

Vinokur turned to face Pikul and Geller. His face wore an expression of relief and pleasure.

"Thank God I got here in time!" he said. "I've been trying to find you." He waggled the cadaver-gun, looking at it and marveling. "My dog brought me this."

"But you didn't get here in time," Geller said simply and obdurately.

"What do you mean?" Vinokur gestured expressively at the body of Hugo Carlaw.

"The game is dead. *eXistenZ* is finished. And it was you . . . you murdered my game."

"No, Allegra, I did not. I murdered your game-pod. The game itself is healthy and happy."

"No."

"I replicated your pod's entire nervous system when I was repairing it. It's standard operational procedure during surgery. Everything that was in the pod at that time is still safe."

"You made a copy of *eXistenZ*? Kiri, you work for Antenna. You know there's a total no-copy rule, backed up by summary dismissal if you break that rule."

"I do."

"Well then . . . how can you stand there and say that!"

"Obviously I couldn't if I still worked for Antenna. That's changed."

He let the significance of those words sink in.

"You're going to defect?" Pikul asked.

"I've already done so. I'm with Cortical now, and it's my happy job to plead with you, Allegra. Come over to join us, come to Cortical Systematics. You too, Pikul. Yes, Cortical Systematics . . . you did hear me right. I've defected and it's the best move I've ever taken in my life. All the Antenna Research top brass are moving with me—Pellatt, Melzack, Sherrin, all the bright and good people."

"So now you're a spy for Cortical Systematics," Geller said coldly.

"Wait a minute!" Pikul had been listening and thinking. He said, "Geller, Cortical Systematics isn't *real*!"

"What?"

"It doesn't really exist. We worked it out, you and I. You must remember! Cortical Systematics is just the game version of Antenna—"

Vinokur cut across him, directly addressing Geller.

"You want your baby back, Allegra. Well, you can have it . . . but the only way is if you come over to us. *eXistenZ* by Allegra Geller. Only from Cortical Systematics."

Geller said, defiantly, "Only from Antenna Research."

She sat down on a rock, close to where Carlaw had fallen. His submachine gun was beside her foot.

"You're intending to hang on, then?" Vinokur said, hefting his weapon.

"I have to."

"But why? Look at that mess down there in the valley. This whole issue of Realism has been completely screwed by them. Everyone involved at Antenna has bungled. If they can't handle what is basically just a PR situation, how good are they going to be when it comes to something really difficult, like marketing *eXistenZ*? Anyway, how can you ever trust them again? They've repeatedly endangered your life."

Geller stared at the ground. Carlaw's arm was curled painfully under his body, his back had humped as he fell.

Pikul looked too. He thought, pitying the man, What a way to go, what a place to die.

"So what do you say, Allegra?" Vinokur said.

"I don't know."

She sounded as if she'd lost the thread of his argument. Absently, she reached down and picked up Carlaw's gun. It looked large and heavy in her hands, and she seemed not to know how to handle it.

"Be careful," Pikul said. "It's probably still loaded."

"Yeah, and it's still cocked," she said.

"Put it down."

"Yeah." Her voice was distant, as if her thoughts were miles away. "You know, this guy Carlaw was actually going to kill me."

"But I saved you," Vinokur said. He turned to Pikul. "Can't you talk some sense into her? I mean, I've already said I would expect you to come to Cortical Systematics too. You'd receive a substantial raise."

"Do they have slots open for marketing trainees?" Pikul asked.

Vinokur was about to answer, but whatever it was he intended to say never made it out of his lips.

In a sudden blaze of violence, Geller pulled the trigger of the automatic weapon. There was a deafening burst from the muzzle and Kiri Vinokur was thrown back onto the jagged rocks. Blood surged from his head, his neck, his chest, his groin.

Geller's senseless and sudden action finally galvanized Pikul. Not caring what she might do to him, defending herself or warding him off, he lunged at her and swatted the weapon out of her hands. It fell to the rocky ground with a loud metallic clatter. He kicked it away from her, then darted nimbly across to it and grabbed it before she could.

"What the fuck are you doing, Geller?" he shouted. "You killed him!"

"He had it coming," she said in an uninterested voice. "He killed *eXistenZ*."

"He said he didn't."

"As good as."

"You can't fucking kill people for stuff like that!" he yelled. "What's next? Are you going to kill me too?"

"Come on, Pikul!" She threw back her head and let out a giddy laugh. "Vinokur was only a character in a game. You worked that out yourself. I just didn't like the way he was messing with my mind."

"You didn't like him messing with your mind. So that makes it okay to kill him?"

"He was only a game character."

"But what . . . ? What if my theory was wrong? What if we're not in the game anymore?"

"We have to be."

"Are you sure?" Pikul asked. "Are you *really* sure?"

"Sure I'm sure. What you said made sense."

"That was only me, trying to explain things. But you know more about *eXistenZ* than I ever will. For instance, what about . . . what about that reality bleed-through you were talking about? That must have happened many times before." She was silent. "Well, has it?"

"Yes."

"And what about D'Arcy Nader?"

"What about him?" she asked.

"The famous game residue. Remember? And he was dead by then!" Pikul waved the weapon in despair. "None of that makes sense anymore, if you can just kill anyone you think threatens your game! And how do you know this is still the game?" he asked. "How can you be sure?"

She looked toward him, and in the still-glowing glare from the destruction in the valley, he could see that her cheeks were streaked with tears.

"We must be," she said, and she drew a deep, shuddering breath. "If . . . if we . . . if we're not?"

"If we're not, Geller, then you just killed someone real. Someone you knew, someone who had been your friend. A real person."

She still did not seem to understand. Pikul felt himself driven to his final argument, the one he'd reserved, always buried in him.

"You've seen what can happen," he said. "It's important for me that you see that."

"Why important?" she said in a dull voice.

"I have to tell you. Now, at last. It wasn't by accident that you and I ended up on the run together."

That finally got her interest.

"Not an accident?" she said.

Pikul raised the automatic weapon in his hands. "No."

He let it sink in.

She stood up, moved to the edge of the declivity over the valley below. She leaned forward, and Pikul thought she might be about to jump. But she swayed a little, then looked back at him.

"You never had a bioport, yet somehow you were working for Antenna," she said. "That's why, isn't it? You were one of them."

"I still am," he replied. "One of them, I mean."

"But you have a bioport now. Why did you get it fitted? I thought that was forbidden to Anti-eXistenZialists."

"Not this one. Well, strictly speaking I had to. It was a great sacrifice, but I had to get close to you. I had to make love to you, to my enemy. A terrible sacrifice."

"Not that bad, I hope."

"No . . . but still a sacrifice."

"Why would you do that?" she asked.

"To best understand the person I was sent to kill."

The new but final realization dawned in her.

"You, Pikul?"

"Yes, me," he said, holding the gun. "I am the one. Understand that."

"No . . . you understand this instead," she said quietly. She pulled what looked like a tiny version of a TV remote control from the flap pocket of her shirt. "Understand that I suspected who you were from the moment you made that fake phone call to yourself in the limo. Understand that I knew you were my real assassin when you pointed the gun at me in the Chinese restaurant. Understand that no one in my position goes unprotected about the world."

She flicked up a safety cover from the top of the remote, revealing a microswitch. She pointed the device at him.

Pikul tensed his hands on the automatic weapon.

"And understand that you're a dead man, Ted Pikul."

Her finger jabbed down on the microswitch, and in the same instant the bioport on Pikul's back exploded into white flame.

He screamed in agony, convulsing and falling. His frenetic jerking spasms threw him to the rocky floor, bashing his head, his arms, his back against the sharply jagged outcrops. He rolled and squirmed, in unimaginable pain.

Geller danced before him, waving the tiny remote above her head.

"Death to the demon Ted Pikul!" she yelled, shouting her laughter across the wide-open valley below.

Pikul, still barely conscious, hardly able to take in anything other than the violent sensations of his own pain, rolled in convulsing spasms toward the edge of the hill. As his vision dimmed, he found that he could see down into the valley. The last flames were now being extinguished. A thick pall of black smoke rolled through the valley, under the bland, uncaring moon-light.

His mind was dying. The last words he heard before the ultimate blackness flooded in came from Geller.

"Have I won the game?" she was crying in child-ish glee. "Have I won? Have I won?"

Then another kind of blackness flooded in around them both.

[26]

It had once been a simple country church, but was deconsecrated years ago. In recent times it had been used for dances, community meetings, elections, the occasional political rally. The hall was typical of the sort of places where game companies took their product out for market evaluation: it was in a remote country area with a high percentile of known game-software users, the hall familiar to everyone in the locality and cheap to rent, and in addition it was an unobtrusive place for the top VR people to gather. You couldn't be too careful these days.

There was a platform, with players sitting on chairs. To one side of them was a blackboard on an easel. Their seats were arranged in a loose semicircle, and some of the principal technology of the game was resting on the floor of the platform in the middle of the players. The rest of the hall was filled with an admiring, eager audience, waiting their own turn to evaluate the brand-new game system being launched that night.

There were two security guards, armed only with electronic wands.

Neither of them was Ted Pikul.

One of the guards had a dog on a lead. It was squatting in a bored fashion beside the man, chewing gutturally on something hard.

Pikul himself was on the platform, hooked into the game. He was a player, who earlier had been selected from the crowd, only too eager to be one of the first to try out the new system.

Allegra Geller sat beside him, one of her hands resting companionably on Pikul's forearm.

Both of them were sitting with their heads tipped forward peacefully. All the other players had their heads tipped forward peacefully.

The audience waited quietly and politely, sipping the glasses of iced tea and chilled mineral water that had been handed out earlier. They were not willing to make any commotion that might precipitate an early end to the game. They wanted to see how this new system worked out on its own. They were going to be next; they all hoped they would be next. These advanced-system game evaluation seminars were legendary for the way in which everyone present was given a turn. No one was left out who wanted to be in.

Even the two security guards would be allowed to put aside their electronic wands and try the system before the evening was out.

No one liked having to wait, though. The suspense was agonizing.

Overseeing the whole event was a woman named Merle. She was not only in charge of setting up and running the seminar, but responsible for the security of the various participants. She was one of the few people there who would not be hooking in to the system that night.

While the game proceeded she kept an eye on the electronic monitors, making sure nothing went wrong from that point of view, but her overall concern was the well-being of the players and what they made of the new system. So she was at her most tense as the game went on, able to relax a little only when it ended.

This was signaled by a general sense of stirring among the players. One of them, whose head had been lolling forward, straightened slowly. Another moved her hand, flexing the fingers gently. One or two people allowed their legs to stretch, or they muttered a barely audible groan of contentment.

Allegra Geller sighed, and her fingers tightened affectionately on Ted Pikul's arm. He grunted.

The VR sets the players were using did not in themselves represent a breakthrough in technology. At seminars like these the company always relied on tried and tested hardware, temporarily retroadapting the game software to work in the old boxes. When the product was eventually launched, it would be accompanied by its own sleek, state-of-the-art tech kit—difficult for the clone-makers to reproduce, at least for a few months—but at this stage plans had still not been finalized for the hardware.

Tonight the players were therefore wearing conventional VR equipment: the traditional large VR headsets, which input data through the optic and aural nerves and other sensations through paste-on electronic sensors.

These headsets were linked by ordinary wires to the game modules, which rested in the players' laps.

Again, the technology was reasonably conventional, the only departure from the norm being a thumb-sensor. This was a recessed input/output aperture in the side of the module, into which the player inserted his or her thumb, where more microsensors translated and evaluated the gigabytes of sensory data the program required or generated.

Seeing that many of the players were stirring, Merle nodded an okay to one of her two assistants. The rather matronly woman stepped into the center of the semicircle and flipped the master switch on the console that stood there.

At once there was a collective sigh from the players. Their eyes fully opened and they looked around at each other, blinking in the lights.

"Are you all back, ladies and gentlemen?" Merle asked, stepping up on the platform. "Is everyone okay?"

There were general sounds of assent, and one by one the players slipped their thumbs out from the sensors and took off their VR headsets.

Some of the women shook out their hair, loosening it after the confines of the helmet, while one or two of the men scratched their sweaty scalps ruefully. No one much liked wearing the VR helmets for long, but at the same time no one much liked breaking out of the game.

One of the first to remove his helmet was the man sitting beside Allegra Geller. It was Yevgeny Nourish.

Nourish put down the VR headset, glanced around at the other players, then leaped to his feet. There was a distinct energy to the man, and he radiated exuberance, artistry, and a dynamic youthfulness. Unlike the game version of himself, Nourish had a shining, almost messianic fervor in his eyes. He wore casually modern clothes, and his dark hair was cut short. He appeared to be in his mid-forties.

"Hi, Merle!" he called, as much for the benefit of the audience and the other players, as for Merle herself. "Yes, we're all back. And safely too, I think.

Although I suspect that some of the present crew might not realize it yet."

Yevgeny Nourish spoke perfect English, without any trace of a foreign accent.

The other players, emerging back into reality somewhat more slowly than Nourish, laughed a little shakily and glanced around nervously at each other.

One of them, a Chinese man with a cheerful face and an athletic body, stretched his arms and back, then grinned around at the others.

"Wow!" he said. "What an experience! Anyone here want a bowl of hot and sour soup?"

The other players laughed, although still nervously.

"Is it on you?" one of them said, a young man in grease-stained overalls.

"Sure thing," said the Chinese man. "Tonight it's all on me!"

That made them laugh louder, and it broke the ice.

"I'll have some soup," somebody else said. They turned to look at him. It was Kiri Vinokur. Again, all trace of accent was gone from his voice. He looked younger, healthier than the Vinokur who had appeared inside the game. "I'll have some," he said, "but only if you can guarantee there will be lots of amphibian mutations in the rice."

"Frogs' legs a speciality," said the former Chinese waiter. "No one from France here, is there?"

They all shook their heads.

One of Merle's assistants took a reading from the central console.

"That was a total of twenty-two minutes and thirty-five seconds," she called across to Merle.

"Right. Thank you."

"Twenty-two minutes?" Another player spoke up. He was a young man wearing blue jeans, a white T-shirt, and a shiny leather jacket. It was Noel Dichter. "It seemed like days when we were in there," he said. "That's fantastic time-dilation. I've never experienced anything like it before."

D'Arcy Nader put down his headset and mopped the top and sides of his head with a huge spotted kerchief.

"If that was only twenty minutes," he said, "think what it could mean if we stayed in longer. If you spent the rest of your life in the game you could live to be five hundred. Not a bad deal!"

Hugo Carlaw was on the platform too.

He said, "Those twists and turns at the end made my head spin. Maybe there were too many plot changes, coming too fast for ordinary players to take in." He looked across at Ted Pikul and Allegra Geller, now both fully awake. "But, hey, you two were fantastic. You guys are game divas! I think you both deserved to win."

There was a burst of spontaneous applause at this,

coming mainly from the other players. The larger audience, of course, lacked the experience of the game and could only guess at what the players meant. But the others on the platform clearly all agreed with Carlaw's verdict.

Pikul and Geller smiled sweetly back, and graciously acknowledged Carlaw's compliments with modest nodding of their heads.

"Well, it's all right for some of you." It was Gas, the young man in the greasy overalls. "Let me be honest with you. I felt really bummed out at first. I was knocked out of the game so soon."

Nourish said, "Yes, I know—"

"But it was only at first I felt like that," Gas went on quickly, wanting to get his say in. "I didn't realize that if you're knocked out suddenly you get to play smaller roles in the later stages. That was a lot of fun for much of the time. I was one of the fire fighters at the ski club, and I'd never been involved in a big fire before. And earlier I liked being one of the spooky customers in the game store."

"I was there too, but I didn't see you." It was Wittold Levi. "But, you know, during that interlude in the filling station, you were wonderfully wicked. The devil gets all the best tunes, right? I had a big part in the first scene at the church hall, but I thought my character was, well, kind of boring, and after that I wasn't given a whole lot to do by the game."

"Yeah, but think what happened to me. I played a gas jockey, and in real life I'm a gas jockey! I was frankly disappointed to be the same thing in a game. I play games to escape from reality . . . so let's have a little more fantasy there, fellers."

Merle had been listening closely to all of this, and she nodded sympathetically at Gas's words.

"You're making an interesting point," she said. "But why not hold it right now, and we can look at it again when we get to the focus group?"

Gas raised his hand from his lap in brief acknowledgment of that.

Frances, a lady with a comfortable manner and graying hair, held up her game module.

"Does anyone mind if I keep the kit?" she said, smiling to show she wasn't entirely serious. "The sensation this little gizmo can give you! I've never felt anything like it! And I love the thumb hole. What a thrill!"

"Nice try," Yevgeny Nourish said, to more general laughter. "But as you know, you're all going to have to turn them in because a lot more people are going to want to try them. Anyway, these modules are just beta-test versions, preproduction handmade specials. We have to take them to pieces after this evening's tests and examine them for whatever wear and tear they've suffered. But everyone here will get a certificate for helping out. That's right, isn't it, Merle?"

"Right!" Merle said. "And anyone who receives a certificate this evening will be granted a privileged order status. That means if you turn in the certificate at your local game store, or at any one of the nationwide mail-order outlets, you can reserve one of the first batch of the production modules to hit the market. The game, of course, is *TranscendenZ* by PilgrImage. You'll be given a discounted price, and I really mean seriously discounted. You're going to love it."

She stepped to the side of the platform, where the chalkboard was standing. She picked up a piece of chalk and with a practiced hand wrote the two words.

"Remember," she said. "It's always written like this. *TranscendenZ* with a capital T, capital Z. It's new, it's only from PilgrImage—capital P, capital I—and it's coming soon."

She gave the blackboard an extra tap with the chalk to lend emphasis to her words, then walked to the front of the platform again, brushing off the loose chalk dust from her hands.

Allegra Geller stood up, placed her module on her seat, and crossed to Yevgeny Nourish. He had his back to her at that moment, so she gently touched his hand with hers. He turned to see who it was and smiled broadly.

"Ms. Geller!"

"May I say thanks, Mr. Nourish?" Allegra said shyly. "I just want you to know how much I appreciate you giving me the chance to play the star designer. I guess the game picked up on my ambitions to be like you."

Speaking partly to Allegra Geller, but also for the benefit of the audience, Nourish said, "Let me be the first to say that I'm kinda glad I lost this game. I don't usually cast myself as such a nasty character."

There was general amusement at this. Allegra joined in the polite laughter.

Nourish took her hand and held it up.

He said to the audience, "This young lady . . . well, this is Allegra Geller. I want to say, Allegra, that you were so good in your role that I suspect it won't be long before PilgrImage is after you to sign a design-ing contract."

A lot of people clapped at this, and whistled loudly.

"And maybe," Nourish went on, "maybe you should take your friend Ted, Mr. Pikul here, with you. You make one hell of a team. Ted's good in a crisis, and when you design games for a living, there are certainly plenty of those."

Allegra actually blushed, and reached behind her for Pikul's hand. He came forward quickly and stood beside her.

She said, "I guess it's no secret that Ted and I had a relationship before we came here tonight. We really do like to play together."

Pikul took up her theme.

"That's right," he said boldly. "But I'd like to assure everybody here that Allegra wouldn't really jump into bed with a trainee security guard unless he were me. Right, Allegra?"

"Right!"

She clung to his arm, while everyone laughed again. The two security guards particularly enjoyed this banter.

Merle stepped to the center of the platform.

"Well, what do we have to say to our designer? Our brilliant, award-winning designer, as I should properly describe him? Does he have another winner on his hands, or doesn't he?"

The wild and prolonged applause from all the gamers gave an unequivocal answer to that.

Nourish took the acclaim modestly and happily, smiling and looking around the crowd. Geller and Pikul were particularly demonstrative of their feelings, and Pikul slapped the man heartily on his back.

Merle finally quieted everything down, raising her hands, and with smiling gestures brought the applause to an end.

"Okay, everyone," she said. "Now we have to get down to business."

Pikul let out a theatrical groan, which Merle neatly acknowledged with another smile.

"I have to ask everyone who took part a number of questions, before the game half-life wears off. But first, let me thank you, every one of you, for contributing to this test seminar. It's part of PilgrImage's ongoing customer satisfaction program to deliver nothing but the finest games to the greatest enthusiasts. Tonight, you have all been a proud part of that process.

"In a moment," she continued, "we'll be collecting all the headsets and game modules. After that we'll be handing out a brief questionnaire to each of you, and we ask you to take a little time to fill it in for us. I want your answers to the questions to be honest, brutally honest if necessary. Don't hold back on anything. As the leading game corporation, we are seriously committed to evaluation and reevaluation, and if you give us clear responses to the game you have just played, we can build on them for the future.

"After that, we'll select the next group to play the game, and the first group will go into focus session, where we can interact on a personal level. We need to hear you talk about what happened to you while you were in *TranscendenZ*. You've had separate experiences inside the game, but they all interlock. The focus session will bring out that interaction. I think you'll find it slightly amazing." She raised her hand to indicate that her speech was over. "Thank you, everyone."

↔   ↔   ↔

After the questionnaires had been handed out and the participants were quietly answering them, Nourish walked over to Merle at the side of the platform. He spoke quietly to her.

"We've got to talk, Merle," he said.

"What is it? Something wrong?"

"I don't know about wrong, but I was more than somewhat disturbed by the game we just played."

"It sounded to me like it was a howling success."

"In some ways. Perhaps not in others."

"What do you mean?" Merle asked.

"It had . . . undercurrents. Violent undercurrents. No, not as remote as that. Violent main themes, and disruptive themes too. We all know that violence is a part of gaming, but . . . "

"Go on."

Nourish looked troubled. "It had a strong antigame theme. None of this was in the main coding. It was . . . out of control, if you like. For instance, it started with the attempted assassination of a game designer."

Merle tried to shrug it off, still not entirely sensing how serious Nourish was.

"Really?" she said. "That's a creative departure."

"Yeah . . . we're programmed for that. The game is designed to allow random events, even unpredictable random events. But randomness in a game is usually positive: a reward, a revelation, a higher level of reality. Starting on a negative like that is not good." He flicked a quick, warning look at her. "It's not to be ignored. The source has to be tracked down."

"When you put it that way, I think I see what you mean." Merle glanced across at the players, many of whom were now quietly working their way down the second page of the questionnaire forms. "I admit that does make me nervous. If it's not in the code, then what's happening? Could it have derived from one of the volunteer players?"

"That's the assumption I'm forced to make."

"Any idea which one of them it might have been?"

"It sure didn't come from me!" Nourish considered for a moment. "The tone of the whole game was passionate, fanatical. There was an atmosphere of paranoia, and the constant sense of betrayal was overwhelming. All the way through it felt unstable, dangerous, volatile. Yeah, I know . . . it's just a game. But worse than that there was a sort of subplot. I never got to terms with any of it. There was a constant theme of industrial espionage, corporate stakeouts were going on, head-hunting, thefts of game systems and company assets, employees jumping ship from one game company to another. That kind of thing."

"Just like the real world, then?" Merle said with a cynical grin.

"Not the real world I live in," Nourish said sincerely. "I was in on PilgrImage from the start. You know that, Merle. I'm as firmly committed to our corporate ideals as anyone can be."

"Sorry." She nodded toward the group of players. "So if it came from one of them, who could it have been?"

"Maybe we could use the focus group for that," Nourish said. "It's clear to me we've been infiltrated here, and if we have, we've got us a big security problem. Let's just get them interacting and see what develops. These group sessions usually throw up a few surprises."

"Okay, I'll handle that. I'll do what I can."

They were interrupted by Ted Pikul and Allegra Geller, who had separated themselves from the main group. Pikul was leading the dog the security guards had been looking after for him while he was playing the game. Both he and Geller were holding their questionnaire forms.

"Hi, Merle," Pikul said. "We were wondering if we could ask Mr. Nourish a couple of questions, away from all the others?"

"Sure, go ahead." Nourish turned on his affable smile. "So long as you don't want me to fill in your questionnaire."

He chuckled, but Pikul was regarding him with great seriousness.

"We've played your game now, Mr. Nourish," he said. "So we can finally agree with the others that you are the world's greatest living game artist."

"Thank you, Ted," Nourish replied.

"We weren't sure before this evening."

"Glad you could be here, then." Nourish was backing off, in no mood now for small-talk.

Allegra Geller said, "Yevgeny, don't you think you should be made to suffer for all the harm you've done, and still intend to do, to the human race?"

"What? Is this a joke?"

"No joke," Pikul said. "Don't you think that the world's greatest game artist should be punished?"

"What for? You're not making sense."

"Punished for the most effective deforming of reality?"

"Okay, I get it."

Nourish turned away sharply, pushing against Geller as he did so. He staggered then, and Geller moved away and leaned downward. Nourish shouted to the two security men.

"Hey, boys!" he yelled. "Could you get over here—*right now?*"

But it was already too late.

As she stooped, Geller was reaching toward the dog standing obediently at Pikul's feet. She touched something on the dog's neck, and immediately two large flaps of false fur and skin folded away from the dog's back. Two semiautomatic pistols were held against the dog's flank.

Geller grabbed them both, and tossed one to Pikul.

She shot Nourish. Pikul shot Merle.

Their two bodies immediately fell to the floor, with a loud crashing of limbs against the wooden boards and the clatter behind them of overturning chairs.

"Death to the demon Yevgeny Nourish!" Geller screamed.

"Death to PilgrImage!" Pikul screamed with her. "Death to *TranscendenZ!*"

Everyone in the hall was immobilized by the sudden eruption of violence in their midst. Everyone, that is, except the security guards, who were weaving quickly through the crowd toward them, their ineffectual electronic wands raised in readiness.

Pikul and Geller took aim at the men, steadying their gun hands with confident holds.

"Stop, or you die now," Pikul said calmly and clearly. "Believe me, it ain't worth it."

The guards stopped in their tracks. They tossed aside their wands and raised their hands, then backed off.

"Okay, there's going to be no more shooting!" Geller shouted. "Unless anyone does anything real stupid! You hear?"

A few people nodded fractionally, hardly daring to move.

Pikul and Geller began to sidle toward the exit, covering the crowd with their guns, switching aim suddenly and randomly, discouraging any interference. They were both pumped up, ready for anything.

Halfway to the main exit they passed the Chinese man. He'd pressed himself nervously against a pillar, with his hands raised. He was sweating copiously. In one hand he held his half-completed questionnaire, in the other he held a ballpoint pen.

Pikul and Geller paused by this man, while they waited for Pikul's dog to catch up with them. It trotted through the room, then headed for the door.

"Okay, now stay real cool," Pikul said. "Anyone makes a sudden move, they die. Got that?"

They continued on toward the door.

Suddenly, the Chinese man unfroze. He lowered his arms and took a step or two away from the pillar. Both guns immediately zoned in on him. Pikul tightened his finger on the trigger.

The man again stopped and raised his hands.

"You don't have to shoot me," he said, sweat pouring down across his eyes. "I just want to ask you a question."

"What?" Geller said.

"Tell me the truth. Tell all of us the truth." He glanced around the crowd for support, but no one else moved or spoke. "This is still a game, isn't it?"

Pikul looked at Geller; Geller looked at Pikul.

"I guess that's something you might never find out," Pikul said.

He and Geller backed out of the hall, into the night, into the darkness. They melted away, disappearing into the greater world of reality beyond.